Kasey's
River Song

Norma Lewis

SPINNING DREAMS IN GOLD RUSH ALASKA

NORMA LEWIS

Publication Consultants Since 1978

PO Box 221974 Anchorage, Alaska 99522-1974
books@publicationconsultants.com—www.publicationconsultants.com

ISBN 978-1-59433-613-3
eBook ISBN 978-1-59433-614-0
Library of Congress Catalog Card Number: 2016933371

—First Edition—

Manufactured in the United States of America.

Prologue

Memories of Da washed over me. He came here first, leaving Mama and me back home until he and Hot Pants staked Claim Five Above on Raven Creek. He said that meant it was five claims above Discovery Claim, the creek's fist.

"Come to Alaska," Da wrote. "Come and hear the river sing. When I asked Mama what he meant, she said we'd soon find out.

Six weeks later the captain had stood next to me on the deck of the *Alice B.* "Listen to that river. She's just a-singing today," he'd said.

First Da, now the captain. Kittiwakes flew overhead and rested on rocks along the riverbank. Sea parrots perching in the trees answered their calls. A loon cried. River water slapped over rocks and lapped the banks. Silvery salmon splashed to the surface.

"I hear it!"

"I see you do." The captain chewed the stem of his pipe and smiled. "Yep, little lady, you'll be happy here. The ones that don't hear the music, them's the ones that ain't.

Chapter 1

The call of a lone loon floating on Raven Creek seemed to beckon me. Not that I needed coaxing. I had hurried through my chores, and a fresh loaf of sourdough bread cooled on the table. Glancing around, I saw that everything was in place. Da's bed stood at one end, with my bunk attached to the wall opposite the windows. Both held a fluffed featherbed and blanket. Two chairs flanked the table, and two more hung from pegs on a moss-chinked log wall. Above the table an unlit kerosene lamp rested on a shelf.

Finally! Creek time. Outdoors after almost two weeks of steady gray rain. When a soft breeze brushed my face I almost ached with joy. All right, I should probably be working on Da's new shirt. And I would. After my bath. Between the cabin and creek I spotted a pile of bear scat, but it wasn't steaming so I didn't worry.

The creek shimmered in summer sun so bright that gravel and small stones on each side sparkled. Crystal clear water flowed above rocks protruding from the mucky bottom. Though only late-August, birch and aspen trees blazed autumn gold. The fireweed was cottoning out on top, and like Alaska's short summer, would soon be only a memory.

I yanked off my black velvet ribbon and shook my hair free, then slipped out of my ankle-length calico dress and undergarments and spread them over a fallen log. Clutching a cake of soap, I dipped one big toe into the creek. *Brrrr.* No matter how many times I did this, it always came as a shock. Shivering, I dunked my whole body. Some people get wet an inch at a time but to me, that's torture. I made my way to deeper water where we had made a dam of rocks.

The loon took wing and I had the creek to myself. Something rustled in the trees, but I saw nothing. *Must have been my imagination.* I lathered my body and ducked under to rinse. Soap scum rose to the surface and floated away. Next I soaped and rinsed my hair.

Someone, or something, trampled the brush again. Closer. With no time to get my clothes, I crouched down behind overhanging willow branches. Water lapped my shoulders.

I waited, but saw no one. Suddenly I saw it. A black bear! He plodded to the creek bank straight across from me and took a drink. We see bears all the time, but this one stood so close I could see dried mud matting his coat and droplets of water on his black snout. Unaware of my presence, he moved a few feet downstream.

What should I do? I thought of throwing a stone in his direction to scare him off. Or yelling at him. No. If he thought he was alone, better keep it that way. To get to my clothes, I'd have to cross the creek again. It might work, but only if he kept moving downstream, away from the cabin.

My heart didn't just hammer, it almost jumped out of my chest, and that bitter taste in my mouth must have been fear.

Moving upstream looked like my best option. Then I could cross over, grab my clothes and run. Or at least get to the cabin without my clothes if I had to. If only my knees would stop shaking.

Ever so slowly, avoiding rocks, and taking care not to splash, I crept farther upstream, still under cover of willows. That's when I heard squirrels chattering in the trees over my head. *"Be quiet,"* I silently begged them. For a moment they did. I held my breath, but they started up again.

That's when the curious bear looked straight at me. I froze. He plunged headfirst into the creek. I'd say I was terrified, but I've been terrified before. This was worse. Much worse. What could I do now? Climb a tree? No. Black bears are tree climbers. No point in running either. I knew I'd never outrun him.

I stayed motionless for a moment or two, and he lost interest. Without another look in my direction, he lumbered out of the water, shook himself a few times, and ambled away.

"ThankGodthankGodthankGod."

My thanks proved premature. He turned around. I stayed locked in place, but he didn't want me, only my dress. First he sniffed it, then clenched it between his teeth and sashayed toward the main trail. My terror turned to anger. "Hey, you thieving beast, that's mine! Bring it back!"

He looked back over his shoulder as if to say, "Try and make me." At least he left my petticoat and unmentionables.

By the time I'd changed into my other everyday dress and brushed my still-damp hair, it was time to start supper. Da's gold mining partner, Hot Pants Hogan, usually ate with us, so I set out a third plate and took his chair from its peg.

Da had met Henry Hogan on the Chilkoot Trail when they both were coming into the country. One night a campfire spark caught Henry's trousers on fire. Da knocked him down and rolled him in snow. He's been Hot Pants ever since.

I warmed the rest of last night's roasted moose meat, along with a big pot of beans, and water for my tea. Then I sliced bread and measured out coffee for Da and Hot Pants.

"Kasey! Kasey! Where are you? Kaasseey!! I heard Da's voice in the distance, hollering my name over and over again, at an increasingly fevered pitch. *Now what?*

"Kasey! Where are you, darlin'? Kasey?" Now Hot Pants had taken up the chant. Even Da's husky, Prince, seemed to be barking more than usual. *What's going on?*

I stepped outside just as they came into sight. Da waved my tattered dress in the air, still yelling my name. Mystery solved: That pesky bear.

"Da, I'm fine," I shouted running toward them. When we met, he held me so tight I could scarcely breathe.

"When we found this... We thought ...." He gave up trying to speak, and trembled against me.

"He didn't hurt me but he stole my dress when I was bathing."

"Goshamighty, darlin', if your pa had met up with that bear, he woulda killed it with his bare hands. I'd a-helped him."

Da still held me in a death grip. When he finally let me go, we were both teary-eyed. Hot Pants hugged me extra hard, and his eyes were red too.

"If you had become that bear's supper I'd never have forgiven myself," Da said.

"If that ever happens, and it won't, you should probably blame the bear."

He tried smiling at my feeble joke. "Saturday we'll go to Bradley Pass and get you cloth to make a new dress. Two dresses. Three. Whatever makes you happy!"

"One dress is enough. Don't you know I'm already happy? Now wash up, both of you. Supper's ready."

I've always called my father Da, probably because that's what he called himself. One of my earliest memories is of waking from a nightmare and Da holding me, saying, "It's all right, lass, Da has you. It was just a dream." He stayed with me until I drifted off to sleep again. "Da" and "lass" were words he brought with him when he left his home in Scotland.

He and Hot Pants sat down to eat while I poured coffee and put our supper on the table.

"No more bear talk," I said. "How did it go today?"

"We're making good progress," Da said. "Tomorrow we might find a vein."

We ate in silence. I finished first because they took second helpings.

"Delicious as always," Da said.

"Amen to that, darlin'," No surprise there. I doubt Hot Pants ever sat down to a meal he didn't enjoy.

I accepted their compliments with a smile, but couldn't help noticing Da looked troubled. *Forget the bear,* I wanted to say, but couldn't after insisting we not talk about it.

Hot Pants left and Da offered to help clean up, but I said no. "You worked hard all day. This is my job," I told him.

"Kathleen Camille…" I could tell he wanted to say something, but couldn't seem to find words.

It sounded serious. He never called me by my real name. Mama named me for my two grandmothers, Kathleen Mackenzie and Camille Bradshaw. Da said my name was bigger than me, so he called me K.C., and the letters soon blurred into Kasey.

"Kasey," he began again, "what happened today made me see how unfairly I've treated you."

"What are you talking about? I couldn't ask for a better father."

"I mean that ever since your Mama died, you've been stuck here keeping house for me."

"Da..."

"Let me finish. You had to grow up too fast and missed your chance to be young and carefree. It's all my fault."

"Why don't you believe me when I say I'm happy?"

"Are you? Or do you think you are because this is all you know?"

"Da, I love you, and I love our life here."

"You're a good daughter, lass. I've been blessed."

Chapter 2

I sat on the same log the bear had stolen my dress from the day before and inspected Da's new shirt. All done but the hem. My tiny, even stitches pleased me, but I wrinkled my nose at the color. Brown. The trading post had only a few bolts of cloth left. All drab. It didn't matter. He needed a shirt, and he liked everything I made.

Mama taught me to sew as soon as I was old enough to hold a needle without pricking myself. I don't think I'll ever be as good at it as she was, but it's something I love doing. Two years ago Mama took sick and died. I know it sounds silly, but sometimes when I'm sewing I feel like she's still with me. This morning when I sewed the buttons on Da's shirt. I could almost hear her saying, *Kasey, don't forget to loop the thread around the shank a few times.*

A dog barking in the distance broke the tranquil silence. *Sounds like Prince. Wonder why Da's coming home so early.* I dashed inside and stashed his shirt under my bunk so as not to spoil the surprise. After lighting the woodstove, I ladled water from a bucket into my copper teakettle.

Prince barked louder. I heard Hot Pants' voice. Then Linnea Amundsen's. Linnea shouldn't be out. She was with child and Dr. O'Malley had ordered bed rest. When her time came closer I would stay with the Amundsens for a few weeks. Linnea was my dearest friend. Except Michael Walensky, of course, and he had been working so hard I'd hardly seen him all summer.

"Kasey! You are here? Ya?" Linnea spoke with a heavy Norwegian accent I'd grown to love.

"In here, Linnea." I ran my fingers through my hair then stepped back out in the warm afternoon sun.

Hot Pants helped Linnea down from the buggy. *Where is Da?*

"There was an accident," Linnea said.

Tears streaked her face. *I don't want to hear this.*

"What happened?" The words left my mouth, but in a voice sounding nothing like my own. "Da's not back yet, but I can help."

"It ...it's your Papa . . ." Linnea's voice faltered.

"No no no no no ..."

"Take me to him," I said aloud, still in that stranger's voice.

Then Hot Pants held me. "Darlin', he's dead."

I knew it. When I first I saw them standing there I knew. I heard their words. Understood them. But this had to be happening to someone else. Hot Pants half carried, half dragged me inside. When the water had boiled, Linnea poured it over loose tea in the bone china teapot Mama brought from Virginia. Hot Pants sat at the small table trying to explain what had happened. I barely heard him.

"... shaft broke ... hit him on the head. . ." I plucked the shirt from under my bunk and began hemming.

"... dead when I found him." Hot Pants still spoke.

Prince howled.

Linnea filled three cups, then gently took the shirt. "Don't, Kasey. Ya, no need for it now."

"If he doesn't wear it now, when will he?" I snatched it back. Oh yes, I saw worried looks passing between them. I saw it all. I just didn't care.

Word flew through our small mining community. Nils Amundsen came. Michael Walensky came too, along with his father, John, his mother, Anna, and older brother, Peter. I knew I should be crying, but why? I'd soon wake up. This had to be a nightmare, because it simply couldn't happen to me. Not again. Nils and Linnea took me home with them.

Hot Pants put himself in charge of Da's funeral, and asked Michael and Peter to dig a grave. They built a coffin, too, and lined it with spruce boughs, but a moose came along and ate the spruce, so they had to gather more.

Early the next morning I heard Hot Pants talking to Michael and Peter. "Go dig another hole, boys, somebody's gone and jumped our claim on this here one."

When I ran to the open grave I heaved. For a moment I was sure I'd faint. Anna Walensky steadied me. During the night someone had placed a stranger in the grave. Da's grave. The man was quite dead, and except for his floppy, oversized orange hat, quite ordinary. No sign of foul play. No bullet holes. No neck burns. Everyone assumed he was a Cheechako, a newcomer, but how did he get there?

"He didn't just happen along and lie down and die," John Walensky said. "Who left him here? More important, why?"

Anna still had her arms around me.

Hot Pants came and laid his hand on my shoulder. "One thing's for sure, darlin', if your pa's watching these shenanigans he's laughin' his head off."

A strange noise gurgled out of me. Half laugh and half cry. Then the tears came. Buckets of them.

"That's right, baby. Let it out. Oh baby, baby, I'm so sorry." Anna rocked me in her arms.

I loved Anna. She had been like a mother to me these last two years. Still, I wished she wasn't there. Because then this wouldn't be happening. I could go back to yesterday morning. Back when to when all I had to think about was Da's new shirt and staying out of that bear's way. Back to when I didn't need all the loving kindness Anna showered over me.

"What am I going to do, Anna? I'm all alone."

"You're not alone, baby. Not while there's still one other person in this gold camp." She held me at arm's length and looked me straight in the eye. "I pray someday you'll be my daughter, but until then you belong to everyone here. Look at me, Kasey. You are *not* alone. I love you. We all do."

"Anna's right." Susannah Prentice had driven her buggy in from Bradley Pass, the nearest town for hundreds of miles. She pulled me away from Anna and wrapped her work-worn hands around mine. "We love you and we need you. In fact I need you to work in my hotel this winter. I can pay you a small wage and give you room and board. Please say you'll do it."

"Susannah, that's perfect. She can work for you until she and Michael get married," Anna said. Then she clamped her hand over her mouth. "Oh dear, I shouldn't have said that. But it's what your father wanted, you know. It's what John and I want, too."

It was true. Da and Anna always joked about grandchildren they would someday share. I still remembered my discomfort whenever *that* subject had come up. Now if I could have him back, I'd let him say anything he wanted to. I wouldn't even blush. Well, I probably would, but just a little.

I helped Anna and the other women prepare Da's body for burial. When Mama died, the women decided I was too young, and insisted Da keep me away. Now at thirteen I had to take on adult responsibilities. Why had no one ever warned me that growing up meant doing something this painful?

We washed him. *He's my father. Will I ever be able to forget I saw him naked? I don't want to remember him that way.* We dressed him in clean trousers and his new brown shirt. *Maybe I shouldn't have made it. Maybe God wouldn't have taken him in his old raggedy shirt.* All right, I knew that made as much sense as Da saying he would have blamed himself if that bear had hurt me, but I couldn't help it.

Suddenly it became too much. My stomach lurched. I knew I was going to be sick again, and dashed outside. Michael found me and held my forehead while I heaved. Then he rocked me as his mother had done. Neither of us spoke. What could we say?

Reverend Watson, the itinerant preacher, was off making his rounds, but what the funeral lacked in formality it made up for in heart. We buried the stranger and prayed for him. Whoever he was.

Then Hot Pants, John, and Da's other friends shared their favorite memories of him. They talked about what a good man Charles Mackenzie had been. They asked God to bless Da, and to look after me. Then we buried him next to Mama.

Chapter 3

Hot Pants took Prince, and I moved in with the Amundsens. Nils put a cot for me in a corner, and hung a quilt for privacy. Cooking and helping Linnea sew baby clothes kept me too busy to think during the day. I even made myself a new green dress to replace the one the bear took.

But every night I stuffed my fist in my mouth so no one would hear me cry. I cried until I thought I'd turn inside out. When Mama died, I didn't think my broken heart could ever mend. But somehow Da and I had managed to make a happy life. Now, no matter what Anna had said, I had no one.

Dr. O'Malley's office was in Bradley, so Anna checked on Linnea often. She mothered everyone, not just me. Hot Pants came nearly every day, too. His mouth smiled, but his eyes looked as if they had forgotten how. Da was like the son he'd never had. I'm ashamed to admit his pain helped ease mine, but it did. It made me feel less alone. As long we all remembered him, Da he would live on through us.

One night Hot Pants stayed for supper. Midway through our beans and bacon, he handed me a moose hide poke containing eight hundred dollars, Da's share of the summer's clean-up.

Nils looked surprised. "But I thought..."

"Eight hunnert," Hot Pants interrupted. "Kasey, darlin', you know I'll keep on giving you your pa's half."

I wrote to Da's mother, Grandma Kathleen, and Mama's mother, Grandma Camille, and broke the terrible news. Both wrote back insisting I come and live with her. I refused both offers.

"Is better you should live with one of the grandmothers," Linnea said.

"Grandma Kathleen lives in Scotland. I've never even seen her. And I'll never go back to Virginia and Grandma Camille. She hated Da, you know. Blamed him when Mama died.

"At least think it over. Ya. Family, it's everything."

"There's nothing to think about. Not now. Not ever."

"Kasey, come quick!" Late one night, Nils called me outside. I wrapped a quilt over my nightdress and ran to join him. A soft glow hung overhead. Curtains of purple, green, and rose crackled across the sky, flashing and dancing until spent. More followed, each brighter than those before.

I could only watch open-mouthed. "The sky is alive!"

"Ya. The Northern Lights they come all the winter long. But never like this."

"What's happening? What does it mean?"

"Things happen, ya, and you never know why," he said. We both knew he was talking about Da, not the lights.

Then Linnea cried out. I ran the whole two miles to fetch Anna, the lingering lights showing me the way. A baby girl came the next morning. Nils named her Aurora.

Anna washed her, then wrapped her in a blanket and placed her in my arms while she tended to Linnea. Aurora's tiny hands balled into fists, and her hair, what little she had, was damp and plastered to her head. I stared at her in wonder, and she stared back. A confused stare, as if she were thinking, "Who are you, and how did I get here?"

I loved her instantly, and wondered about a birth following so soon after a death. Was that God's way of easing pain? One thing I did know. As soon as Linnea regained her strength, I had to move on.

"Michael, talk to me or I'll scream." We were halfway to Bradley Pass, and all I'd heard for at least a half hour had been MacBeth's and McDuff's plodding hooves.

"Sorry, guess my mind wandered." He patted my hand, but still stared straight ahead. "Feels like it's getting colder. Heard there'll only be one more riverboat before freeze-up."

"For heaven's sake, Michael, stop. This is Alaska. We both know it's getting colder." I hated this new awkwardness between us. I hated crying, and I hated being cried over even more. *Why Da? Why did you leave me like this?*

"I don't know what to say to you. It's all so unfair."

"D-Da . . ." I stumbled over the word. "Da always said life isn't fair." *He sure had that right.*

"I worry about you, that's all. We all do."

"Well don't. I have a job and a place to go. You're my best friend and you're acting like you don't even like me."

"If I didn't like you I'd make you walk to Bradley Pass." He tried teasing, but I refused to let him get away with it.

"You would not, and anyway, I'd rather walk than ride with you when you're acting like this. Can't we go back to how it used to be?"

"What do you mean? Nothing's changed."

"Everything's changed! Before the accident you hardly slowed the buggy for me. I almost had to run along beside you and jump in. Today you fussed over me like I'm an old woman." I flung off the caribou lap robe, but the biting wind forced me back under it.

"Do you *really* want to work in Susannah's hotel?"

Had he lost his mind? I *really* wanted to go home and find Da there. Mama, too, while I was wishing. But I gave him credit for trying. "For now, yes. Come spring, who knows?"

"Whoa," he said, and when McBeth and McDuff stopped, he took my hands in his. "Kasey, don't do it. Let's get married."

"Married? I don't know what to say."

"That's easy. Say yes."

Why not? A lot of girls married at thirteen. Da had expected us to marry. Anna and John, too. But did Michael really want to? For that matter, did I? When I tried to imagine us living together in the cabin Da built, I couldn't. Mama once told me not to marry until I loved someone so much it hurt to be away from him. Like she had loved Da. She didn't think twice about moving to Alaska. Even when it meant leaving the only home we'd ever known, and alienating Grandma Camille. I didn't love Michael like that. Not yet.

"Neither one of us is ready for that," I said. "Someday, maybe, but not now." *Da's death is my problem, not Michael's.*

"So maybe it's not quite the right time. Now's when you need me." His words sounded sincere, but I had already seen relief on his face when I said no.

No wonder he'd been so quiet. He had probably agonized over this for weeks. I almost laughed, but kissed his cheek instead.

"I do want to get married someday, and when I think about it, the girl is always you," he said.

"Of course, silly. You don't know any other girls."

"It's more than that. A lot more."

"I know. I think about you that way too. But we don't have to figure it all out today."

I'd watched him begin a freighting business last spring, right before his sixteenth birthday. He took mail and supplies back and forth between Bradley and the mines scattered along the creeks. He said gold mining wasn't for him. "A man can work like a mule all year and still come up empty at clean-up. I want a sure thing," he'd said.

He had poured all of his energy into making it work, and so far had not had to go to work the family mine with John and Peter. That pleased me. He called mining uncertain, I called it dangerous. Michael clammed up again. I tried thinking about my job, but I'd never had one before , and that made it hard.

We soon reached Bradley Pass and Front Street on the Yukon River. It was far from a real street, however, more like a wide muddy path. The new Alaska Commercial Company general store now stood where been an old trading post had been. A few saloons and cafes that had started out in tents now operated out of log buildings. Every man I saw had his collar turned up against a cutting wind.

A flutter of excitement tickled my stomach as Michael hitched his horses in front of the Golden Nugget Hotel. *This is my future, and it's starting now!*

"Keep your ears open," Michael said. "Maybe you'll find out who he was."

"Maybe." I shuddered. I still couldn't bear to think of that dead man we found after Da died. I still had nightmares about him and his ugly orange hat.

"Well, I guess this is it," Michael said.

"Yes." I couldn't say more. My voice would betray me, and I refused to cry. Little girls cry, not almost-grown-up ladies with real jobs. My prior excitement had completely vanished.

Michael opened the door and put my bag inside. Then, as if sensing my apprehension, he took me in his arms and kissed me. I kissed him back, and my stomach fluttered again. I realized we had never kissed full on the lips before. It felt good. All right, it felt better than good.

"I'll stop by whenever I can, so don't you go marrying anyone else." His earnest gray eyes and crooked smile reassured me.

"I'll try not to," I said, and even managed to smile back.

In the dining room two grizzled miners sat in a corner wolfing down caribou stew. Susannah and another woman drank tea at a small table in the middle of the room. I couldn't see her face but something about her seemed familiar.

Susannah smiled, then turned to her guest. "You won't be needing a ride to the creeks after all. Here's Kasey now."

The older woman stood and turned. No! It couldn't be. "Grandma Camille!"

Chapter 4

I stood for a moment, unable to move, then ran and embraced her. We rocked back and forth, wet cheek to wet cheek.

"Grandma!"

"Oh child, it's so good to see you! I've missed you so much." Grandma stepped back and looked at me. "You're the picture of your mother. You're taller, but you have her blue eyes."

It was wonderful seeing Grandma, too. How long had it been? Four years. She looked smaller than I remembered. Older too. How difficult a journey it must have been for her. First a train to Seattle. Then sailing to St. Michael. And finally, a riverboat up the Yukon. I basked in the long-forgotten scent of English lavender wafting from her black woolen dress.

"What are you doing here?"

"I've come to take you home."

"But I *am* home." I stiffened, as I remembered why I hadn't seen Grandma for so long.

"Never mind that nonsense," Grandma said. "Your father should have sent you to me after your poor mother died. I wrote and told him to, you know.

"I know, Grandma. He showed me your letter and told me it was up to me. I wanted to stay here. With him."

"Well you can't stay now. Even he would agree with that."

"Grandma . . ."

"Kathleen Camille, we won't argue. Your ticket is in my carpetbag. When that riverboat gets back here on Wednesday, you and I are boarding it."

"Pardon, Ma'am, guess you ain't heard about the *Alice B.*," one of the miners interrupted. "She's iced in up at Fortymile."

"Then we'll wait for the next boat. When will that be? Thursday? Friday?"

"That's just it, Ma'am. *Alice* was the last one this year. Now she's iced in."

"He's right," said the second miner. "Won't be 'nother one till May. You know, breakup. When the ice goes out."

"Are you telling me I can't take my granddaughter out of this wilderness until May?"

"Yes, Ma'am. That's a fact."

"Well, land sakes, there has to be another way."

"Only if you want to ride several hundred miles on a dog-sled and then climb the Chilkoot Pass."

Grandma's face paled. I eased her back onto her chair.

"Susannah, it looks like I won't be working here this winter after all." Then I turned to my grandmother. "I know it's not what you had in mind, Grandma, but *I'm* taking *you* home." I bent down and kissed her cheek.

Ice! Glorious ice! I willed myself not to jump up and down. Now I had all winter to figure out a way to stay here.

My head spun. There was chopped wood at the cabin, but how much? And what about food? Da shot a moose and three caribou right before he died. We had winter meat. I had put up carrots, peas, and cabbages, along with wild blueberries and cranberries. It was all packed away in the cache. We could buy flour and staples like dried apples and beans here in town. I couldn't wait to go ice fishing and add cod to our larder. If nothing else, we would feast.

I found Michael at the Sourdough Café.

"You'll never guess what happened. My grandmother is here and she's iced in. Can you please take us to my cabin?"

"Stay with Susannah tonight," he said. "It's almost dark and the weather's getting worse. I'll have Hot Pants start a fire for you tomorrow. Fetch water too."

It's funny how things happen. I had come here to start a new life. Grandma's arrival changed everything. But while it would be good having her here this winter, I knew one thing for sure. Come May, when she went back to Virginia, I would stay right here.

"How far away is your house," Grandma asked later.

"Not too far, but it'll take two or three hours to get there."

"I wish I had enough money for us to stay here at Miss Prentice's hotel, instead of traipsing all over creation."

"It'll be all right, Grandma. We'll be warm and comfortable, and we'll have plenty to eat. You might even like it."

"I seriously doubt that. But I've learned one thing since the War of Northern Aggression, and that's to accept what I can't change."

Grandma still used the old Southern term for the Civil War that had changed her life. My grandfather died at Manassas. Before that, they had been part of the comfortable, but not wealthy, merchant class. The way Da explained it, an impoverished South had created a genteel poor class, not to be confused with those known by the derogatory term, poor white trash. Old rules of society remained rigid, even while a new South still worked at righting its wrongs.

We had just sat down for lunch in the dining room the next day when I saw him. A stranger glanced my way and a hint of smile flickered in his brown, almost black, eyes. He looked to be in his early twenties, and handsome in a city sort of way. Emily Duncan, a dancer at the Gilded Cage, sat drinking coffee at the table he had just left. She looked troubled, but whatever had darkened her face disappeared when she saw me.

"Kasey Mackenzie!" She jumped up and ran to hug me. "I heard you were coming. It'll be so nice having you here this winter. I hope to see a lot of you."

"I would have liked that too, but my plans have changed. Grandma, this is Emily Duncan. Emily, meet my grandmother, Camille Bradshaw. Grandma is staying with me until breakup."

"Pleased to meet you, Ma'am. You must be Rosemary's ma."

"Emily helped take care of Mama when she took sick."

Grandma looked as if she had guessed Emily's occupation, but being a southern lady, she politely hid her disapproval.

"That was kind of you, I'm sure, but she needed a hospital. Would've had one too if she hadn't run off to Alaska."

"Uh, yes." Emily squirmed. "Well I'm glad you'll be living here with Kasey, especially now that Charles is gone too,"

"I don't plan to live here. Come spring, Kasey and I will be leaving. This winter is merely an inconvenience. And a mighty big one at that."

I cringed. *It's going to be a long winter. Even by Alaska standards.*

Chapter 5

Michael came for us after lunch. I introduced them, and he carried Grandma's carpetbag outside. I picked up my own bag and followed. That's when I collided with someone wearing a heavy gray coat.

"Pardon me, I wasn't paying attention," I said.

"My pleasure." Two arms steadied me and I looked up into the amused eyes of the stranger from yesterday. I immediately thought of my carrot-colored curls sticking out from under my knitted hat. Some days I remembered to tie my hair back in a velvet ribbon. More often, like today, it fell free.

"Allow me." He took bag.

"I'll take that," Michael said, using his free hand to snatch it away.

"Ladies." The stranger tipped his hat before turning away.

What's gotten into Michael? His apparent jealousy was almost funny, and I have to admit, flattering. All right, the stranger's attention pleased me too, but I wouldn't let myself think about that.

We all climbed in Michael's buggy, Grandma in the middle. This time I accepted the lap robe without complaint.

Piercing wind blew even colder than yesterday. A parcel at my feet reminded me this was a workday. Maybe that explained Michael's rude behavior.

"I feel terrible that you're getting behind schedule because of us," I said.

"Don't be silly. Tomorrow's another day." Now he sounded like the Michael I knew and loved. Oh yes, I did love him, just not yet in a marrying way.

"Michael runs his own business," I explained to Grandma.

"Smart young man. A business is a sure thing. Not like digging holes in the ground for gold that might not even be there." *Please, Grandma, don't start on Da. Not today.*

"Funny you said 'sure thing.' That's what I always say. Not my father and my brother though." Michael smiled at Grandma. "They named their mine the Sure Thing. Said they'd make a miner out of me yet."

"And is it?" Grandma asked.

"Is what?"

"Is your family's mine a sure thing?"

"Mrs. Bradshaw, when it comes to gold mining, there's no such thing. They're doing all right. It's paying. So far."

Late-afternoon sun setting on snow-coated hills tinted them the same pale pink as the dogwoods that bloom in front of Grandma's house. Alaska's splendor astonished me even in its winter starkness. I imagined seeing it for the first time, as Grandma was. Could she see its beauty?

Memories of Da washed over me. He had come here first, leaving Mama and me back home until he and Hot Pants filed Claim Five Above on Raven Creek. That meant it was five claims above Discovery Claim, the first one staked. "Come to Alaska," Da wrote. "Come and hear the river sing. When I asked Mama what he meant, she said we'd soon find out.

Six weeks later the *Alice B's* captain had stood next to me on the deck. "Listen to that river. She's just a-singing today," he'd said.

First Da, now the captain. Kittiwakes flew overhead and rested on rocks along the riverbank. Sea parrots perched in trees answered their calls. A loon cried. River water slapped over rocks and lapped the banks. Silvery salmon splashed to the surface,

"I hear it!"

"I see you do." The captain chewed the stem of his pipe and smiled. "Yep, little lady, you'll be happy here. The ones that don't hear the music, them's the ones that ain't."

Michael's voice interrupted my daydream. "Mrs. Bradshaw, look! Over there." He pointed to a moose lumbering through a stand of Sitka spruce.

"Mercy! I had no idea they grew so big. Do they come up close to your house?"

"They sure do, Grandma. Bears do too."

"Bears?"

"They're hibernating now, but Kasey and I'll teach you how to share this land with all these critters."

Grandma opened her mouth, then seemed to think better of it, and remained silent.

"Did Kasey tell you about the bear that stole her dress while she was taking a bath in the creek?

"You bathe in a creek?" she asked in a horrified voice.

"Only when it's warm enough."

"In a *creek?* Outside? Naked?"

"Grandma, no one saw me but the bear and I'll tell you all about it later." I've always been cursed with blushing, and even today's chill couldn't stop my cheeks from flaming. .

"Naked? Well land sakes if that doesn't beat all."

Michael looked amused. I just wanted to stop talking about nakedness. Especially mine.

We turned off the main trail and onto one more narrow. Another moose crossed our path, but this one had a purple fedora tied to his rack. Grandma grabbed my sleeve. Her eyes bugged.

"That's Stonewall Jackson," Michael said. "Hot Pants makes him wear a hat so no one shoots him. You know, thinking he's winter meat. Makes him work too. Come spring, if you want a garden plowed, Hot Pants and the general will do it for you."

A slight smile tugged Grandma's lips, but her voice was firm. "Kasey and I will be gone long before anything has time to grow. And that, young man, *is* a sure thing."

No point in worrying about that now, I had all winter. Relaxing, I looked out over the countryside. This was our Alaska. Mine and Mama's and Da's. Most miners came into the country to grab the gold and run. Others, like Da and his friends, saw Alaska as a new frontier. They believed Alaska would be a state some day, and intended to be counted among its first pioneers.

I cherished memories of long winter nights when candles made dancing shadows on our cabin walls while we Mackenzies spun our dreams. Now, Mama and Da were both gone. I had no idea how I'd live the life we'd planned, but knew in my heart I'd find a way.

Chapter 6

Just ahead, friendly smoke spewed from my chimney. Hot Pants had a fire going. He'd probably chopped more wood too.

"Whoa, boys," Michael said to the horses. "We're here."

"This is it? This is your house? Land sakes, there's not another house in sight."

"I know, Grandma. That's how it is up here. Hot Pants' cabin isn't far. You just can't see it because of all the trees"

My cabin stood in a clearing. It had a sod roof, and logs chinked with moss. Da's snowshoes still hung from an eave. Two windows were nothing but three rows of empty pickle jars. It probably didn't look like much to Grandma, but I loved it. Home!

Though the woodpile looked big enough to heat all of Alaska. I knew it wouldn't last through Christmas. A log cache on stilts protected our food from marauding bears. An outhouse stood a little ways behind the cabin, but we only used it in good weather. A "honey pot," a porcelain vessel that had to be emptied every day served those needs when it turned cold. I admit that emptying the honey pot is my least favorite chore.

"Kasey, darlin'! Welcome home!" Hot Pants appeared from behind the cabin, ax in hand, his beard laced with ice.

I ran and hugged the big bear of a man. "Hot Pants! Come meet my grandmother. Grandma Camille, this is Hot Pants–Henry Hogan"

"Mr. Hogan, thank you for looking out for my granddaughter until I could get here."

"Call me Hot Pants, Miz Camille. We ain't formal up here."

"Never. I shall have to call you Henry."

"I reckon that'll do. Iffen I can 'member to answer."

Then, before Grandma could protest, he scooped her up and headed for the cabin.

"Stop it this instant, you fool! What do you think you're doing?" Grandma kicked and spluttered. "Put me down!"

"No, ma'am. Snow's pretty deep, and you're dressed for a tea party. Speakin' o' tea, I got water boilin' inside."

"Well, land sakes, you could have warned me."

I faked a cough so Grandma wouldn't see me laugh.

The one-room cabin was exactly as I'd left it. Looking at it, I felt as if a knife had pierced my heart. Da's canvas pants and his old work shirt still hung from a peg. How flat they looked. How empty. Even so, the cabin glowed with cheer. A kerosene lamp burned bright on the table, and tempting food aromas reminded me we hadn't eaten anything since our early lunch at Susannah's.

Hot Pants hadn't just boiled water. Beans simmered on the stove, sourdough bread cooled, and he'd even brought us some smoked salmon. Anna had sent a blueberry pie for dessert. It looked like a feast to me, but I wondered how Grandma would react.

She surprised me. "Michael, if that pie is half as good as it looks, you mother must give me her recipe. I do hope I'll have a chance to make her acquaintance while I'm here."

"It's better'n it looks, and bear lard in the crust is what does it," Hot Pants said. "How 'bout a week from Sunday? To meet Miz Anna, I mean." He turned to Michael. "Preacher sent word he'll be here then."

I could hardly wait. We don't have many occasions to celebrate, and now we had two on the same day. Aurora's christening and Peter Walensky's wedding.

"My ma can't wait to meet you. Rosemary was like a sister to her," Michael said to Grandma.

"Thank you, but we'll have to decline. It wouldn't be proper with Kasey still in mourning"

"Things is different here," Hot Pants said. "We don't get many chances to git together, so when we can, we do. It's simple as that."

"That's not simple, indecent is what it is. Kasey's father has been dead less than three months. What would people think?" Grandma warmed to her argument.

"He ain't gonna get any deader if Kasey goes to a party. And if you wanna get folks' tongues a-waggin', just go ahead and snub 'em."

"He's right, Grandma," I said. "And I have to go. I'm Aurora's godmother."

"I see I can't argue with all of you."

"Glad that's settled. Darlin', if your grandma don't forget she ain't still in Virginny, this cabin's gonna feel awful small by spring."

"Go easy on Mrs. Bradshaw," Michael said. "We want her to like it here."

After supper he put on his mackinaw. "Better be going. I have to hit the trail early tomorrow."

"I'm going to git, too," Hot Pants said. "But I'll look in on you ladies tomorry."

Later, I carefully unfolded a white handkerchief linen christening dress I'd made for Aurora. It had tiny tucks across the yoke, and white ribbon and lace trim.

"It's lovely," Grandma said. "Your mother taught you well."

"Just like she said you taught her. I loved making it. We all adore Aurora, and so will you."

That night, while Grandma snored softly in Da's bed, I tossed restlessly on my bunk. The eight hundred dollars was mine. Da earned it. But what about next year? And the year after? I'd gladly sell my half of the mine but no buyer had come along, and so far it hadn't paid enough for Hot Pants to buy me out.

Images flooded my mind of wood to chop, water to fetch, and fish to catch. *If I ever get to sleep I'll probably have nightmares of chopping wood,* I thought. But sleep, when it finally came, brought only dreams of a handsome stranger with mocking eyes.

Chapter 7

The special day dawned bright and crisp with no new snow. Grandma and I hurried through a breakfast of bacon, bread, and applesauce. Hot Pants had promised to call for us early, so we had little time to dress in our best.

"When we get back to Richmond I'll see about getting you a proper corset. Hard to believe you don't already have one."

"I don't need one, Grandma. And even if I did, I've never even seen one in the general store." I ignored what she said about Richmond.

"You could have ordered one from Sears and Roebuck. Young ladies need corsets."

I laced her into hers and vowed I would never wear anything that uncomfortable. Did she really think I could chop wood and fetch water in such a contraption? I brushed her silver hair, plaited it, and wound the braid into a bun atop her head. She dabbed lavender toilet water on her wrists and neck. Her purple Sunday-go-to-meeting dress might have been frayed in spots, but she looked lovely.

Grandma then helped me dress. I had washed my petticoat the night before and dried it over the woodstove. It smelled a bit scorched, but was at least clean. She slipped my new green dress over my petticoat and buttoned it.

We were ready and waiting when Hot Pants came a few minutes later. Grandma donned her bonnet and gloves. I grabbed Mama's good gloves and my stocking cap. Usually I wore work gloves and a man's trapper hat with ear flaps.

"I wish you had a better hat," Grandma said.

"I don't need one,' I said. "My stocking cap is warm and my parka has a hood."

"Warm is one thing, fashionable is quite another," she replied. I could have told her that fashionable hats were as scare as corsets up here, but didn't bother.

They were at it again. Why did the two people I loved most dislike each other much?

"I had my doubts about this. And if I'd known we were going to a saloon, well let me tell you, Kasey and I would have sent our regrets and stayed home." Grandma complained non-stop as we jostled along in Hot Pants' buggy. His horse, Elwood, seemed determined not to miss a single bump.

"Ain't nothing wrong with the saloon. We have preachin' there ever' time Reverend Watson comes through.'

"That's right, Grandma. Clancy's is the only place big enough to hold us all."

"Well I guess that's to be expected. In a place like this."

"Toads and crocodiles! Can't you go through one whole day without pitchin' a fit over one fool thing or another?"

"Where I come from gentlemen don't speak to ladies in that manner."

"You ain't where you come from, and we ain't ladies and gentlemen. We's just folks strugglin' to do the best we can."

"I'm wasting my breath talking to you. Henry Hogan, you are incorrigible."

"You think if I got a bit more corg'bul you could quit flappin' your jaws? How 'bout it Kasey, think I can?"

"You might could." I laughed. "But I don't think I'd like you that way."

A smile started spreading across Grandma's face, but she stopped it in its tracks. *How does she do that?* Hot Pants *was* incorrigible, but also kind and gentle. Why couldn't she see the generous spirit beneath his rough exterior? Thank goodness we didn't have far to go. My head pounded.

Michael met us at the door at Clancy's. "Something's wrong," he said. "Reverend Watson isn't here. He should have been here an hour ago."

Worry grabbed me. This was Alaska. I pictured a dozen different possibilities. All bad. "Let's not panic yet." I tried to smile. "He'll be here soon."

About thirty people were already there, and a few more straggled in. Without the preacher, nobody knew what to do. The Amundsens and Walenskys had planned on late morning preaching, followed by Peter's wedding, then lunch and Aurora's christening After that, we would have dancing for as long as anyone cared to stay. That's when Clancy would bring out the beer and liquor bottles he always tucked away during church business. Grandma and I added our raisin pie and caribou casserole to a growing abundance already in place atop the bar.

"Something must have happened to him," George Baker said.

"Probably just weathered in somewhere. He'll be along shortly," John Walensky said.

Dakota Joe chimed in. "What if, God forbid, something did happen? It'll be at least spring, and who knows how much longer, 'fore we can get ourselves another one."

"We can have the christening another day," Nils said. "Ya. Whenever Reverend comes this way again."

"As long as it's before Aurora outgrows her beautiful dress Kasey sewed," Linnea said. Concern etched her face.

The wedding held more urgency. Betsy Robbins, had been Peter's childhood sweetheart. They wrote to each other after the Walenskys came to Alaska, and fell in love by mail. When Peter proposed, she left her teacher's job in Idaho and sailed on the *Alice B.* with Grandma. She had been staying at the Golden Nugget and was running out of money.

I wondered if she could have the job I had planned to do. After thinking about it, I realized Susannah offered it as a kindness to me, not a pressing need of help.

If Reverend Watson didn't show up, Betsy would have to stay in town all winter. They couldn't go Outside to get married until breakup. *Outside* is what we call everywhere else.

"Seems to me like somebody here can hitch these younguns. Let's call a miners' meeting and elect someone to git the job done," Hot Pants said.

I had heard of miners meetings. When the seasoned miners, called sourdoughs, first came into the country, anyone who had a gripe called a meeting. Everyone attended and the majority ruled.

"Don't know as anyone ever got married at a miners' meeting," John said. "But that doesn't mean it can't be done."

No one seemed to know if a miners' meeting marriage would be legal, or more important to the bride at least, moral.

"Under the circumstances we should do it. If need be they can go Outside next spring and get it done again," John said.

"Ya. Let's yust do it and be done," Nils said.

So far Peter had said nothing. Nor had Betsy, who appeared close to tears. She turned to me. "You aren't married yet, Kasey. Would you?"

"I don't know," I replied truthfully. I thought of marriage sometimes. All right, I thought about it often, but until Michael's proposal, it had always been something vague and far away. "No," I said, finally. "I want a real wedding."

"I'm not sure I agree," Grandma said. "Naturally I'd rather see my granddaughter married at home, *my* home in Virginia." She looked from Hot Pants to me as if daring either of us to contradict her. "But land sakes, isn't a wedding just two people promising to love and take care of each other? And making that promise in front of witnesses. Doesn't the Bible say, 'whenever two or more of you are gathered in my name, I am there.' Wouldn't that apply to Betsy and Peter?"

Hot Pants stared at her. Speechless. For once.

"Hear! Hear!" Someone shouted.

I wanted to shout too, "Listen, everybody, that's my grandmother!" Instead I put my arm around her waist. An hour earlier this same woman had balked at attending a wedding held in a saloon.

"It's not what I dreamed of," Betsy murmured, as a flicker of hope spread across her face, "but when you put it like that . . ."

Peter took her hand. "We do love each other, and we will take care of each other. And what other choice do we have?"

Betsy hesitated a moment. "You're right," she said, "Let's do it, but you must all promise never to tell my father."

"So it's settled," Dakota Joe said.

"Now who's gonna do it? I say the honor goes to John, the father and the father-in-law," Hot Pants said. After a chorus of yeses and nods, he continued. "Now let's make us up some pretty words. Somethin' lovey-like."

John, Hot Pants, Nils, and George huddled together and set about composing a ceremony, their work punctuated with occasional raucous laughter. Betsy blushed.

Grandma raised her eyebrows. "Betsy, my dear child, what have I gotten you into?" she asked.

Soon the men rejoined our anxious group. Peter and Betsy stood facing John.

First Betsy read the lines she'd been given:

"I came to Alaska to start a new life,
and be Peter Walensky's loving wife;
The preacher's not here, but we have a ring,
We love each other, and that's everything."

Then Peter's turn:

"I'll love Betsy always, and our children too,
I'll always be kind and faithful and true.
I'll protect my family through all kinds of weather,
And we'll always be happy if we're together."

Peter kissed Betsy and slipped the ring on her finger

John concluded the ceremony:

"Now he's her husband, and she's his wife,
We pray they'll have a long, happy life.
He's a miner and she's a teacher.
They're as married as if we'd had a preacher."

All three signed the paper George had drawn up on the back of one of Clancy's receipts. John kissed his new daughter-in-law and shook his son's hand. Anna kissed all three of them, and then Michael. Soon she was kissing everyone.

"The next wedding will be yours and Michael's," she said when she got to me.

I flushed crimson. *Did Michael hear? Does he think I've been telling people he proposed?*

I quickly looked around. No, George had cornered him to talk about a supply order. Grandma hadn't heard either. She sat in a far corner cooing at Aurora and laughing with Linnea.

Midway through lunch, the door burst open, letting in an icy blast of frigid air. There stood Reverend Watson. But I barely noticed. My eyes were riveted on the man at his side. The stranger from Bradley Pass.

Chapter 8

"Sorry I'm late, folks. Should've been more careful. The ice broke when I crossed the Yukon a few miles downstream."

With my heart turning somersaults I only half heard his words.

"Two of my dogs went in," Reverend Watson went on. "Managed to save the other four, and the sled. Lost my pack, though, and didn't have matches or kindling. Would've died of the cold if it hadn't been for Thomas here."

Thomas. So that's his name. When I looked at him again, he met my gaze. I blushed and looked away, willing myself not to look his way again. *What's happening to me?*

"So, my friends, meet Thomas Frye, the man who saved my life,"

"It was nothing," Thomas said modestly. "Just lucky I happened along when I did. Lucky, too, I had matches. Got a fire going and dried the reverend's clothes. And here we are. Sorry to bust in on your party."

"Nonsense. We're honored to have you," Anna said. "Now get some food. Both of you."

After they filled their plates, Thomas squeezed in between Susannah and Michael, directly across from me at one of the plank and sawhorse tables. He boldly looked at me again, and I didn't know whether to be annoyed or flattered. And why couldn't I have gotten Mama's shining auburn hair instead of a carrot-colored mop of curls?

"I've never known a girl named Kasey before," he said, then began singing. "Casey would waltz with the straw-berr-y blonde and the band played onnn …."

Oww. That stomach punch again. It still happened every time a memory of Da caught me unaware. "My father sang that song to me when I was young. I used to think he made it up for me."

"Really? When you were young?" He smiled. "I can see that now you're old."

"That's not what I meant." My face warmed with an all-to-familiar blush.

Michael watched me squirm, but said nothing.

After lunch, Reverend Watson preached a short sermon before officially marrying Betsy and Peter. Then Nils picked up his sleeping daughter.

"What is this child called?" the preacher asked.

"Aurora Kathleen," said Nils.

I flushed, with pleasure this time, not knowing until now that Aurora's middle name was Kathleen.

"It seemed right she should have her godmother's name," Linnea said.

"Ya, Kasey. Don't know what we'd have done without you during Linnea's confinement," Nils added.

The Amundsens, and Peter, who had been chosen godfather, and I stood with Reverend Watson. Everyone else gathered behind us.

Reverend Watson called Aurora a blessing to our community. He quoted Scripture and prayed for her health and happiness. Everyone said the Lord's Prayer, then the Apostle's Creed. Peter and I promised to fulfill our responsibilities as godparents. Finally, Nils handed Aurora to Reverend Watson who sprinkled water on her head. Aurora woke and smiled angelically.

"I christen thee Aurora Kathleen Amundsen, in the name of the Father, the Son, and the Holy Ghost."

Later, while Clancy and Nils took away the planks and sawhorses to make room to dance, I caught Thomas watching me. Michael glared at him making me feel a wave of tenderness for him. He looked so ill at ease, a little too big for his dress-up clothes.

When Dakota Joe and storekeeper, Benny Bennett, picked up their fiddles and began playing dance music, Thomas, not Michael, reached me first. I trembled when he pressed the small of my back as we glided easily together. I wondered where he had learned to dance so well. He smelled of tobacco and damp wool, odors I usually hated. Now both seemed pleasant. Intoxicating even.

"So you're really Kathleen. How did you come to be called Kasey?" he asked as he twirled me.

"I was named for my grandmothers. Camille is my middle name. My father called me K. C. when I was a baby"

"It suits you. I like it." Then his face clouded. "Mackenzie. I've heard that name. Wait. Wasn't that the gentleman who died here last summer? Was he. . ."

"Charles Mackenzie was my father. Did you know him?"

"Never had the pleasure. Must have heard someone talking about him is all. My sympathies."

"Thank you."

He suddenly seemed preoccupied. *It's the same old thing, he feels sorry for me.*

"Now Miss Kathleen Camille Mackenzie, it looks like the Walensky boy's nose is out of joint. I'd better share you."

I couldn't read his face. What had made him so anxious to get away from me? I felt cheated. He had told me nothing about himself. Michael started toward me, but Hot Pants beat him.

"Come on, darlin', let's show 'em how it's done," he said.

Dakota Joe and Benny were playing a crowd-pleaser, "There'll be a Hot Time in the Old Town Tonight." I usually enjoyed Hot Pants' antics, but my mind wandered. His voice brought me abruptly back to reality.

"…dontcha think?"

"I'm sorry, Hot Pants, I didn't hear you."

"Cuz you wasn't listenin'. I said the boys are playin' in fine form tonight. Don't tell me this weddin' business is makin' you and Michael want to get hitched. Toads and crocodiles, you ain't neither one o' you dry behind the ears."

"I'm not thinking about getting married." It came out sharper than I intended.

"Sorry, darlin'. I was only funnin' with you."

"Do you know him, Hot Pants? Thomas Frye?"

"Don't tell me that's who's got you actin' like this."

"I'm not acting like anything. Just curious."

"Can't say as I know him, but somethin' 'bout him don't set right. Seen him 'round Bradley some. Believe it wuz at the Gilded Cage. That satisfy you?" He raised his bushy eyebrows and it looked as if a pair of caterpillars inched up his forehead.

"I suppose. Thanks."

"You're welcome. That grandma o' yours dance?"

"I doubt it, but you can ask her."

"Mebbe I will," he said, spinning me with a flourish.

Grandma and Hot Pants didn't dance, but I finally danced with Michael. Though I tried concentrating on the music and following his lead, I kept stumbling. *Thomas dances so much better.* I saw him watching us, and it felt like his eyes were burning a hole in me.

"Sorry," I mumbled as I stumbled again. I hated that Thomas had seen my clumsiness.

"Pay attention," Michael said. "And stop watching that Cheechako."

"I'm not watching anyone, I'm looking for Grandma."

"Well, you're looking in the wrong direction. Your grandma's helping my ma put out more food."

"I should have known." I forced a smile, but don't think it took.

"Kasey, don't get taken in. I don't know why, but I don't trust that smooth-talking Frye–if that's even his real name."

"That's not fair! You don't even know him. Or do you?"

"No. Just a hunch."

The music stopped and I ended the conversation by pretending to want tea. Flora Baker approached me as I filled my cup from an ornate Russian samovar. Clancy had bought it in Sitka, a remnant from when Russia owned Alaska.

"Kasey, Aurora's dress is lovely. I didn't realize how beautifully you sew. Would you make a dress for me?"

"Yes, of course, if you really think I can."

"I know you can. You decide on a fair price."

Grandma appeared with our coats. "We'll leave now, Kasey. That old fool Henry Hogan will most surely stay until all hours. George and Flora kindly offered to see us home."

Reluctantly, I set the cup down and slipped into my parka. I'd have preferred to stay, but at least I wouldn't have to argue with Michael anymore. And I'd probably never see Thomas Frye again. Though even as I thought it, I hoped it wasn't true.

Chapter 9

Only three days until Christmas. Funny thing is, I'd been dreading it. How could Christmas even happen without Da? Now, with Grandma here everything had changed.

We needed fish for our holiday feast. At first light, around ten o'clock, I bundled up in my beaver parka and mukluks and set out down our narrow trail to one that led to the deeper Pine Creek. First I sawed a hole in the ice, then baited my hook with bacon fat and sunk my line. I soon had three tomcod, close to three pounds each. Hot Pants promised to bring ptarmigan, a grouse-like fowl for Grandma to stuff and roast. Both promised a welcome change from moose meat and caribou.

"Kasey Mackenzie, what a pleasant surprise." I jumped. I'd been lost in my thoughts. Between that and the sharp wind whistling through the aspens, I hadn't heard Thomas Frye approach on horseback.

"Good morning," I said, happy to see him, even though I hadn't dressed for callers. I had pulled my hair together like when I do a single braid down my back. But instead of braiding it, I'd only twisted it and stuck it under my earflap hat. When I removed the hat my hair would look like a bird's nest. Or worse.

"I wondered where you live. Is that your cabin just down that trail? He dismounted and eyed my catch appreciatively. "Looks like you had good luck."

"Yes! Aren't they beauties? But I'm finished now. Won't you come in for a cup of tea? I'd offer coffee but we're all out. Can't get more until the first supply boat next spring." Self-consciously I gathered up my fish and gear.

"I'll give you a hand," he said. He tied my bucket to the pommel. Then he led the horse by the reins as we strolled together. "You're pretty isolated out here. What am I talking about? The whole blooming territory is isolated."

"I know," I said. "Isn't it beautiful?"

"Beautiful? More like wretched. What's a girl like you doing here? You should get rid of that mine and go home. You belong in the comforts of a civilized world. I know I can't wait to get back."

"I've lived in your civilization and I'd rather be here." *What's wrong with him? How can he not see this is the loveliest place on earth?* Maybe he hadn't been here long enough to appreciate it. With some folks it took time.

A few minutes later, Thomas tied the reins to Da's hitching post and took my bucket of fish. We found Grandma baking sourdough bread. "Thomas Frye! Come in," she said. "The tea is steeping, but please don't look at my mess. This cabin isn't big enough for me to keep it neat while I'm working."

"Think nothing of it," he said. "Compared to mine, it's a castle."

While Grandma cleared one end of the table for our guest, I poured the tea and divided the last of a dried-apple pie into three slices.

"Kasey and I were just talking about how isolated we are in this endless wilderness. How about you, Mrs. Bradshaw? What brought you here?"

"Kasey brought me here, but we'll not be staying. We're iced in now, but we'll leave just as soon as possible."

I winced, but said nothing. *No point in arguing with Grandma today. Especially in front of a guest.* I thought of asking him to join us for Christmas, but didn't want to seem forward. This whole "gentlemen caller" business made me uncomfortable. Michael didn't count. I'd known him since I was nine.

Also, Hot Pants would spend Christmas with us. He didn't like Thomas, and I knew better than to think he would try to hide it. Grandma said he was as coarse as a cob. I wouldn't go that far, but a little tact wouldn't hurt him.

"Mrs. Bradshaw, now that I know where you live, I hope you'll allow me to come back often," Thomas said, after we had finished our tea and pie.

"We're always happy to have company, aren't we, Kasey?"

"Yes." Then to keep from sounding forward, I added, "There's not much to do here in winter." *Now he thinks I want to see him because I'm bored.* I felt myself blush.

"You may be sorry you said that, but I'll try not to make a nuisance of myself." He smiled at me, that half smile that always made me wonder what he was really thinking. "Thank you for your hospitality, but I really have to go now. Need to get to Bradley Pass before dark"

"It'll be nice having him visit," Grandma said, after the door closed behind him.

"He probably won't come back."

"Nonsense, child. He likes you, and he seems well bred. Blood tells."

"He did know about the mine," I admitted. "So I guess he asked about me."

"Land sakes, Kasey, don't you ever look in a mirror? Any young man would be interested in you."

"Grandma, do you think he sees me as a girl or a woman? Never mind, don't answer that." I smiled at my foolishness.

She smiled back, then changed the subject. "What we need is a tree. A real Christmas tree."

"Yes! Let's find one. At first it didn't seem right having one without Da, but now I think it's a wonderful idea."

"Your father and I had our differences, but I know he'd be the first to want you to have a happy Christmas."

"I know." Unshed tears burned my eyes. I still missed him so much.

"Do we have enough candles?"

"No, but Hot Pants is going to town tomorrow. He can bring us more."

"Well, of course," said Grandma. "We'll have to put up with that old fool on Christmas anyway, so let's put him to work."

"Grandma, how can you say that? He's always doing nice things for us. Besides, he's always here on holidays. It wouldn't feel like Christmas without him."

"I, for one, could do very well without him. But whatever makes you happy."

"Come on, you know you enjoy him. Without Hot Pants, you'd have no one to argue with." I'd almost grown used to their bickering.

"Maybe so. I guess he's good for something, if only helping me sharpen my tongue," Grandma said with a twinkle.

We tramped out in the snow. Mama's parka fit Grandma. Her mukluks did too, after we stuffed muslin in the toes. We had to hurry. Days were really short now, only four or five hours long. Even then, daylight often looked more like twilight.

"I declare, it almost feels warm," said Grandma, breathing in the crisp air.

"That's because there's no wind. I love days like this, don't you?"

"I can't go so far as to say I love them, but it's sure enough easier being here than I thought it would be."

In the short time we'd been together we had become a family. To my amazement, Grandma had adapted to wilderness living, almost seemed to relish it. She had even taken over emptying the honey pot.

"I'm glad. I know you didn't plan on staying here all winter, but, Grandma, I'm so happy you're here."

"So am I." Grandma's eyes brightened. "Look! There's a perfect tree."

The Sitka spruce had short, silvery blue needles, and would fit nicely in the cabin. Permafrost prevented roots from going down more than a foot or two, making all the trees spindly. I swiped it a few times with my ax and the five- foot tree toppled over.

We dragged it home and stood it upright in a bucket. Then we added water along with a few chunks of wood for support. I reached under Grandma's bed and retrieved a box of corks Mama and I had painted gold the first year we were here. But when I picked one up, it crumbled in my hand.

"We need new ones," I said. "These have frozen and thawed so many times, they're little more than dust. Hot Pants can stop in a saloon and get some more."

"That errand should bring him pleasure," Grandma said.

Hot Pants brought our supplies on Christmas Eve day. "Here you are, ladies. Hope this'll do the job." He gave us candles, gold paint, and a poke full of corks.

"Lord have mercy, you must have paid a visit to every saloon in Bradley Pass to get so many," Grandma said.

"Dang right, I did," Hot Pants said. "Got me a lot of friends I had to have a Christmas drink with." He winked at me, but I already knew he didn't mean it. Everyone around here knew better than to drink too much and then hit the trail. Especially in winter.

Hot Pants also brought two plump ptarmigan and stayed long enough to help Grandma clean and pluck them.

I flattened an empty maple syrup tin, then carefully traced and cut out a star. I painted the star and the corks gold. While the paint dried, Grandma and I made three pies from wild blueberries I'd gathered and put up last summer.

Later, using large needles, we put threads through the corks, and hung them from the tree's branches. The tin star went on top.

Grandma tied on a dozen candles, taking care to keep them upright. She stepped back and inspected our work.

"All done," she said, smiling.

"No. Something's missing. Cranberries! I'll string some."

All right, if I'd known how hard it would be, I probably wouldn't have bothered. The cold, hard berries were almost impossible to poke a needle through. By the time I finished, my fingers were pricked and stained with juice and blood.

"It was worth it," I said, as I draped the string of berries on the tree.

"Our tree is perfect," Grandma said.

This time I agreed.

Chapter 10

Hot Pants arrived early Christmas afternoon. He and Grandma seemed to have called a truce in their ongoing war. I suspected that neither wanted to spoil my holiday.

We exchanged presents before tucking into our feast. I'd bought a lace fascinator for Grandma. "I hope you like it," I said. "It was hard to choose something at the general store, knowing you have so many fine shops at home."

"It's lovely. I'll wear it now." Grandma knotted the scarf around her neck, its creamy lace adding a festive touch to her purple dress. "I'll wear it proudly when we get home, too."

I refused to let the 'when we get home' dampen my spirits on Christmas. Grandma liked her gift, and nothing else mattered. It would have been nice to have made something for her, but keeping it a secret would have been impossible.

I'd made a warm woolen scarf for Hot Pants, and on impulse, made one for Michael, too, and hoped he would stop by.

"Thank you, darlin,'" said Hot Pants, running his knobby fingers over the soft black and gray wool. His voice was tender, matching the look in his eyes." I can't remember nobody ever makin' sumpin 'jest for me."

"Hot Pants, are you ever sorry you never had a family?" I asked, then immediately regretted the foolish question.

"I got me a brother and two sisters back in Georgia. Ain't seen 'em in years. Fact is, I been thinkin' of going Outside next winter to visit."

"Won't that cost a lot of money? I asked."

"Course it will, but I've squirreled away a bit. And you can't never tell, might strike it big next summer. Far as a wife and younguns, after I met up with your pa, and you and your ma got here, I felt like I had me a family. A mighty fine one too."

My eyes stung and when I looked at Grandma, hers were damp, too.

"Toads and crocodiles, don't you go a-feelin' sorry for me. That's the price I paid for bein' a rambler. And for your information, it wuz worth it."

He gave me a box of chocolates, and had a two-pound sack of coffee from his own supply for Grandma.

"Coffee's scarce as feathers on a bull moose, so I reckoned you was prob'ly missin' it," he said.

"Thank you. I've missed it sure enough." She rose to make some. "That first cup will taste like the best I've ever had."

"Don't go makin' it now. It's for you."

"Land sakes, what good is having something special if I can't share it?"

Grandma gave Hot Pants a tin of tobacco, and handed me a small package." I wasn't able to buy you anything. Couldn't find a thing I thought you'd like that day we went to Bradley. But I want you to have this."

I opened a small velvet pouch and took out a gold locket. "Oh, Grandma, it's beautiful. But it's yours."

"It *was* mine. Now it's yours. Your grandfather gave it to me. Open it. He put that picture of your mama in it right before he went away to war. He loved that girl."

I'd never seen a picture of Mama when she was that young. The little girl staring solemnly from the sepia photograph looked exactly as I had looked as a child.

"Thank you, Grandma. I'll treasure it always." I gave her a big hug and kiss. "Maybe you'd rather not talk about it, but what happened when my grandfather left?"

"Well, first he went to Seven Pines. He wrote that the Confederates were successful and the whole unpleasantness would soon be over." Her voice sounded far away as she continued. "Then first thing I knew I received word he'd been wounded at Manassas."

"Musta been awful for you, Miz Camille," Hot Pants said.

"It was. My own mama was still living then, so I left Rosemary with her. I went to take care of my man and to bring him home."

"Then what happened, Grandma?"

"Well, he died before I ever got there. I'd been a fool to think I'd bring him home. He never had a chance. But that hospital, such as it was, had so many wounded men and not half enough help, so I stayed and helped nurse them."

"That was mighty kind o' you. I got myself shot during Sherman's march, so I know the boys 'preciated it."

"Hot Pants Hogan, did you fight the Yankees?"

"Course I did. The Georgia mountains is in the south, ain't they? We didn't go along with slavery, but when Yankees came shootin' at us, we shot back. We might not be book smart, but we ain't stupid either. And watch out, Miz. Camille, you start callin' me Hot Pants, and folks'll start thinkin' you're sweet on me."

"As I was saying," she went on as if he hadn't spoken, "it was the least I could do. Maybe the only useful thing I've ever done. After a few months I went home and raised my Rosemary."

"Grandma, I'm so glad you're here with me, and not alone this Christmas."

"I am too, child. And I really mean that."

"No one should be alone today. I thought about Emily Duncan this morning. We should have invited her for Christmas."

I also thought of Nils and Linnea enjoying Aurora's first Christmas. All right, if I'm going to be honest, I wondered about Thomas Frye too. Was he alone?

"Don't go worryin' yourself none 'bout Emily. Saw her at the Gilded Cage when I went to get your corks. She sent her love."

"I hope she's not alone."

"Don't reckon she is. She acted funny when I asked 'bout her plans. Wouldn't surprise me none if she's got herself a fella."

"Good for her," I said.

"Come to think of it, I saw that Cheechako, Thomas Frye, in Bradley. Believe he wuz at the Cage too."

My cheeks burned when he mentioned Thomas's name. I hoped no one noticed.

"Let's have our dinner, now," Grandma said. We sat at the table and bowed our heads as she said grace. "Thank you, God, for the gracious plenty you have given us on this Christmas. Bless us and keep us. Amen."

She had stuffed the ptarmigan with sourdough bread and dried apples, then roasted them until the skins crackled. I baked the cod and topped them with tinned butter. Even the peas and onions, also tinned, tasted delicious.

After we finished, I cleared the table of everything except coffee and pie. Barking dogs announced company coming. Michael.

"You're just in time for dessert," I said, giving him a quick hug.

"Merry Christmas, everyone" he said. "Just a small slice, please. I'm stuffed fuller than the wild goose Ma made for our dinner, but that looks too good to pass up."

"Nonsense," Grandma said. "You're a growing boy. Have some coffee to go with it."

"Thank you, Ma'am, and my ma sent you a cake," he said, setting a rich yellow cake stuffed with walnuts and cranberries beside the pie.

"Well bless her heart. You must take one of these blueberry pies home," said Grandma.

"Merry Christmas, Michael," I said, and handed him his scarf. I suddenly felt shy. We had never exchanged gifts before.

He seemed pleased and quickly opened the package. "Thank you. This will feel so good while I'm mushing between here and Bradley," he said as he ran his hand over the soft wool. "I have something for you, too."

I opened the small package he handed me, and found a beautiful silver thimble inside. "Michael, it's perfect. I love it."

Midway through dessert another visitor came.

"Merry Christmas," Thomas said, shaking snow from his gray coat. "Hope I'm not intruding

Chapter 11

Thomas also bore gifts, a sack of walnuts and another pound of coffee for Grandma. He gave me a hair ornament made of black ribbon and two bright blue feathers. But he brought more than gifts, tension rode in on his shoulder.

"You came from the direction of Bradley," Michael said. "Is that where your place is?"

"My cabin's on Fish Creek, a little off the main trail."

"What 'xactly do you do there?" asked Hot Pants. "You a miner? And why ain't we seen you before this winter?"

"No. Can't say that I mine. Though that's why I came here. Came up last spring to work a claim with my uncle. "

"On Fish Creek? Ain't no gold there."

"You're right. My uncle, Dave West, staked north of there. In the Tanana Hills. Creek didn't have a name and he didn't bother giving it one. By the time I got here, he knew it was worthless."

"Dave West? Never met up with him, but I know the name," said Hot Pants. "Ain't he one of us old-timers?"

"He *was*. Fact is, he thought we'd have better prospects down toward Fortymile. We packed up and headed out but he took a fever and died on the way. Figured I'd stay this winter and see what opportunities presented themselves."

"What kind of opportunity are you looking for?" Michael eyed him suspiciously.

"Don't rightly know. Though in the last few days this place hasn't seemed quite so bad. But I won't be staying long. This country isn't for me." He looked at me. "I'd like to make some money and go back to Ohio. Start some kind of business. Put down roots."

He wouldn't have shocked me more if he had thrown cold water in my face. "Ohio! Why would you want to go there when you can be here?" I wanted to know.

"Because life is easier there. You don't have to work from morning till night just to survive," he replied.

"What I'm wondering is, if it's so good back there, why did you ever leave?" Michael sounded like he was accusing Thomas of something.

"Enough of that kind of talk," Grandma said. She reached for a match. "It's Christmas!"

I extinguished the two kerosene lamps, and candlelight bounced of the gold corks and star while shadows danced across the wall behind.

"It's beautiful." I hummed, then began singing softly. "Si-i-lent Night. Ho-o-ly Night. . ."

Everyone joined in, even Hot Pants. Nothing mattered anymore except Christmas and our celebration together. Grandma handed Thomas a cup of coffee and a slice of Anna's cake.

"Thank you, Mrs. Bradshaw," Thomas said. Then he turned to me. "Ever been to Ohio?" he asked.

Before I could answer, Michael rose. "No more for me, thanks, Ma'am," he said. "I have to be going."

"I hope I haven't caused any trouble," said Thomas, after the door closed behind Michael. But I saw that mocking half-smile. He not only knew his presence had created friction, he had enjoyed every minute of it.

"You didn't start no ruckus, but don't get no ideas about Kasey an' Ohio. She's a Northerner clean through. Like we say up here, the country's got 'er," Hot Pants said.

When I went out to fetch more firewood, Thomas jumped up to help.

"The Walensky boy resents me," he said while we plucked wood from the pile.

"I'm sorry he was rude. I'm sorry Hot Pants was too."

"Well I think I can understand Walensky's behavior. The boy's jealous." Before I could protest, he spoke again. "Hogan's another matter. Can't figure out what's eating him." His eyes narrowed. "Unless maybe he's hiding something and he's afraid I'll find out about it."

"Like what?" I suddenly felt uncomfortable.

"Like maybe he's holding out on you."

"That's ridiculous. He was my father's partner, and the best friend my family ever had."

"Oh, I don't doubt his affection for you. But at least think about it. From what I understand you're his partner now. Greed makes men do strange things."

I laughed. "Save your concern. So far the mine hasn't yielded enough to fight over."

"How do you know?"

"I know because up until the middle of August my father worked it all day every day."

"But how do you know Hogan didn't strike it big after that and not tell you. Then he could buy you out at a low price?"

"If that's true why hasn't he made me an offer? I won't listen to you talk about him like that." I picked up an armful of wood, then spun around and marched into the cabin.

Thomas scooped up another armload from the neatly stacked pile and followed.

The candles had burned dangerously low, so I relit the lamps, then snuffed out the candles. If I kept busy maybe I could hide my anger from Grandma and Hot Pants. *Who does Thomas Frye think he is?*

"What's troubling you, Kasey," Grandma demanded. *So much for hiding anything from her.*

"Nothing, I'm just tired. It's been a long day."

"Yes it has," agreed Thomas, rising to leave. "Thank you ladies, and you, Mr. Hogan, for sharing your holiday with me."

I handed him his gray overcoat. He faced me and mouthed "I'm sorry" before giving me a smile, a real one this time. One that crinkled the corners of his dark eyes and tingled my spine.

Grandma insisted he take some leftover food. She wrapped some for Hot Pants too.

"Guess you're sayin' it's time for me to go, too, and it is," Hot Pants said, proudly wrapping his new scarf around his neck. "I'll see you tomorry or the day after."

"I'll see you soon, too," Thomas said.

Later in bed, I felt torn. How could I be friends with anyone who suspected Hot Pants of cheating? He did apologize, though, so I should probably forgive him.

Chapter 12

Two days after Christmas I woke up feeling like something good was about to happen. By midmorning, I had tidied up and fetched water. My anticipation turned to restlessness, so I filled the teakettle, more for something to do than the tea itself. Someone knocked on our door.

Thomas. He hadn't wasted any time. But instead of Thomas, Susannah Prentice and a woman I'd never seen before stood smiling in the doorway.

"Susannah! It's good to see you." I hugged her and hoped my disappointment didn't show.

"Kasey, I'd like you to meet Mary Schmidt," Susannah said.

"It's a pleasure. Please, come in."

The short, plump woman smiled. "I'm delighted to meet you too, Kasey. I've heard so much about you. But you're even younger than I thought you'd be."

"This is my grandmother, Camille Bradshaw."

Grandma was already pulling out the table to make room for our guests.

"We've met," Grandma said. "Mrs. Schmidt and I sailed together last autumn."

“That’s right. I remember now. But weren’t you were going right back home?”

“So I was, but that’s another story.” She smiled and took four cups from the shelf.

“Mary came up to join her husband and now she needs a couple of dresses,” Susannah said.

“I didn’t bring much. Thought it would be easier to buy new things once I got here. Do you know there isn’t a dress shop in Bradley Pass? Not one.”

“That’s why we’re here,” Susannah said. “Mary admired Flora’s dress and wants you to sew for her, too.”

“Would you be willing to do that? And what about hats? Do you make hats? Does anyone up here make hats?”

By the time they left, I’d promised to make two dresses and try fashioning a hat. I had a seed of an idea. Though it didn’t seem like it now, winter would eventually end. Then Grandma would try to make me leave. Maybe she’d relent if I proved I could take care of myself.

For months I’d worried, and the answer had been right in front of me. Most women could sew if they had to, but I excelled at it. Not only that, I loved it. If I could figure out how to make hats, I could easily make a living. Maybe even open a shop in Bradley some day.

As if reading my mind, Grandma spoke. “What about hats, Kasey? Have you ever made one?”

“No. I never even thought about it until today. Mama did, though. She brought some millinery supplies with her when we first came up here. I remember she made and sold a few.”

“Perhaps there’s something left.”

“Let’s look. Da put most of her things in his trunk after she died.”

We dragged his heavy trunk away from the wall where frost had rusted its lock. I managed to pry it open. Under Da's woolen trousers and two heavy canvas shirts lay a white envelope, addressed to Da in blue ink in Mama's neat script. I felt a stab of the familiar pain.

"What's this? It's Mama's handwriting," I said. I opened the envelope and found two letters inside. "Grandma, listen. These are letters Mama and Da wrote to each other just before we came here:

My dear wife and daughter.

Join me in Alaska. Come and hear the river sing. The cabin is built, and the mine is starting to pay. We may never be rich, but the gold is there, and we will have enough. I know this is my dream, not yours, and I love you all the more for sharing it with me. Should you be unhappy here, I promise we will leave at the end of one year. Enclosed is money for your tickets. I'm sending enough to bring your mother too if she will come. She might not like Alaska, but let's let her see for herself. Anna Walensky will write and advise you on what to bring. Fondly, Charles.

My voice quavered as I read Mama's reply.

Dearest Charles,

Kasey and I will join you as soon as possible. I long to see the face I have missed for so long. Anna wrote and said I can probably earn money making hats as they are in such short supply she has taken to wearing one only in the worst of weather. Thank you for inviting

Mama, but she refuses. I can't wait to see the land where a moose wears a hat while ladies go bareheaded. Kasey and I will sail aboard the Victoria *on the first Sunday in June. From St. Michael, Alaska, we have booked passage on the* Alice B. *It will seem like forever until we're all three together, a family again. Your loving wife, Rosemary.*

Grandma gasped. "Oh, Kasey, I was a stubborn old fool to make my daughter choose between her mother and her husband." She dabbed her eyes with a lace-edged handkerchief. "And your father. I never gave him a chance. I know he was a good man or she wouldn't have loved him. And you wouldn't be the girl you are. Can you ever forgive me?"

"Of course, Grandma. And Da would too. He never held a grudge against anyone."

"My beautiful daughter. It breaks my heart that she died not knowing how much I loved her." Grandma's voice broke as tears gushed. "I thought we had plenty of time to make our peace. She found happiness here, except for worrying about me. The first day I walked in this cabin, I knew it had been a happy home. I could feel it."

"Mama knew you loved her. And she loved you. She used to talk about all of us going Outside. Going down to Richmond and bringing you back."

We looked through the rest of the things but found nothing for hats except a few strands of brightly colored velvet and grosgrain ribbon, Mama had saved an advertising circular bearing the name of Miss Carolina Wilson of Richmond, Virginia, who sold custom-made hats and millinery supplies.

Chapter 13

Thomas visited the next day, and almost every day for the next two weeks. He never mentioned Hot Pants again. Then one afternoon while helping me fetch water he said, "I'm really sorry for upsetting you on Christmas."

"I'd rather not talk about it." I handed him the ax.

Because I drew water from the same place every day, only a thin layer of ice had formed. Thomas quickly chipped through it and filled one of the two buckets. Then he faced me. "I know how fond you are of Hogan, but be sensible."

"He would never, ever, take anything from me!"

"Then at least ask him about it. What proof can he show that you got your fair share, or that you'll keep on getting it?"

"He's never done anything to you, why do you hate him so much?"

"I don't hate him."

"Then why are you doing this?"

"Don't you know? For you. For us."

"Us?"

He put his hands on my cheeks and pulled me toward him, then gently pressed his lips against mine. My heart beat so loudly, he must have heard it.

"Kasey, you have to know I care about you. If we were to get married, I'd stay here and work your mine with Hogan. But not without being absolutely sure he's been honest with you."

Thomas cared about me. As a woman. He almost said he wanted to marry me. So why did I still feel apprehensive?

"Don't you understand? We have to know for sure.

"If it'll make you happy, I'll talk to him. But you'll see I'm right." I dipped the second bucket in the stream. Marry Thomas? I shivered and didn't know if it was the cold or something else. Neither of us spoke as we trudged back. Once inside, he acted as if the kiss and whole conversation had never happened. Grandma eyed me curiously when we entered.

"Do we have any more raisin pie?" I asked, a little too brightly, hoping to ward off her questions.

Grandma served the pie. Hot Pants stopped in before we finished eating.

"Afternoon, ladies," he said. "Frye. Spendin' a good bit of time here, ain't you?"

I knew he still didn't like Thomas and here I was in the middle, just like with him and Grandma.

Thomas only smiled. "You could say that, though I could say the same of you. But where else could we enjoy the company of two such charming ladies?"

"Can't argue with you there, young fella. Least one of em's charmin'. Other one could be iffen she put her mind to it."

"Land sakes, who'd want to waste her charm on you? Why that would be like putting perfume on a pig." Grandma handed Hot Pants a cup of coffee and put the last slice of pie on a clean plate for him.

"Grandma! You're as bad as he is."

"Never you mind, darlin'. Long as she keeps on a-feeding me her raisin pie, she can say anything she jolly-well pleases."

Thomas laughed. "I hate to leave such a stimulating conversation, but I really have to be on my way."

"Come back soon," Grandma said.

"Try and keep me away. Kasey, don't forget."

"Don't forget what?" Grandma asked.

"Nothing," I said. *If only that were true.*

I decided to talk to Hot Pants before he left and get the whole unpleasant business over with. Then Thomas would see how silly he had been. All afternoon I fidgeted and wondered how to bring it up.

Hot Pants noticed my discomfort. "What's the matter, darlin'? Never seen you act so nervous-like. I don't git that undone when I'm waitin' to see how much pay dirt I have at cleanup."

I bit my lip and plunged in. "Hot Pants, how *do* you know how much pay you get?"

"That's easy. I weigh it. Then I take it to the Alaska Commercial Company and they weigh it again and pay me for it."

"Do they give you a receipt?"

"Kasey!" Grandma looked shocked. "What are you saying?"

"I reckon I know what she's gittin' at. If there's sumpthin' on yer mind, spit it out. Otherwise it's time for me to git." He tipped his chair over on his way out.

"Hot Pants! Wait!" But the only response was the door slamming behind him.

"What's come over you?" Grandma asked.

"I wish I knew." Tears filled my eyes. Did he leave because I hurt him, or because Thomas had been right? Just having that thought pierced my heart.

A half hour later Michael burst in, his face red with rage.

"Pardon me Ma'am, for barging in," he said to Grandma. He turned angrily on me. "I just met Hot Pants on the trail. He said you accused him of cheating you. Did you?"

"I didn't *accuse* him of anything. I just asked him some questions."

"Hold on a minute, Kasey, are you telling me you actually believe Hot Pants would cheat you? That's crazy."

"Well, maybe not. Else why did he leave in such a huff? I know if he did anything wrong, he plans on making it up, but how do I know he got what he said he did?"

Even as I said it I didn't believe it, but a scene kept repeating itself in my mind. Last fall, when Hot Pants gave me my money, what had Nils started to say, and why had Hot Pants interrupted him?

"Thomas Frye! That's who's putting those ideas in your head. You should be ashamed of yourself. Kasey, can't you see that Cheechako for what he is?"

"And what might that be?"

"A troublemaker, an opportunist, and who knows what else."

"He only wants to make sure I get what's mine. He cares about me."

"Sure he does. What lazy drifter wouldn't care about a pretty girl who just happens to own half a gold mine?"

"It's a lot more than that. But you wouldn't understand. He's a man. You're still a boy."

"A boy? Was that a boy who proposed to you when you were all alone in the world?" His voice trembled with anger.

"I'm sorry, Michael. I'm not that girl anymore."

"You sure aren't. I liked her. We meant something to each other. What happened to that?"

"I'm sorry, Michael, but there's no use talking about it. You just don't understand."

"You're right. I sure as heck don't! Sorry again, Mrs. Bradshaw." For the second time that afternoon our door banged shut.

I flung open the door, but Michael didn't look back. He stood runners of the sled, then yanked his Christmas scarf from his neck and stuffed it in his fur parka.

"Hike," he called to his team, and the barking dogs left a wake of swirling snow.

Chapter 14

Each passing day tightened a growing knot of misery in my stomach. I never meant to insult Michael by calling him a boy. His marriage proposal had been a kindness I still cherished. But why did he have to be so obstinate about Thomas? Michael had no reason to question his integrity. Far worse, I had deeply hurt hot Pants. The aroma from his pipe still lingered, a constant reminder of what I had done.

"Grandma, what am I going to do?"

"Mercy, child, don't come asking me." She finished rinsing our stockings and hung them over the stove to dry. "I'm never going to interfere in anyone's life again. You'll just have to follow your heart."

"My heart doesn't know what to do. I think I'm in love with Thomas, but why am I so miserable?"

"Life is like that sometimes, honeychild," Grandma said.

"I feel so bad about questioning Hot Pants. Da trusted him completely and so should I."

"Well, I'm not going to commence giving advice, but I'll tell you one thing. Henry Hogan may be a cantankerous old goat, oh, let's not sugarcoat it, he is cantankerous old goat. But I don't think there's a dishonest bone in his body."

"I'll make Thomas stop at Hot Pants' cabin on our way back from Bradley this afternoon. It's time to apologize," I said.

"You do that, Kasey. Take it from an old fool, you never know when it's going to be too late."

"Grandma, I'm so glad you're here. I need you."

"Bless your heart, I'm happy to hear you say that, but you don't need me. I used to think so, but truth is, I need you."

"We need each other. Please come along with us today."

"Thank you, no. I declare it's gotten so cold if you don't eat fast, the beans freeze between your plate and your mouth."

"You're exaggerating." For the first time in days, I laughed.

"Maybe. But not much. I'll just stay here and try to keep my bones from shaking."

I'd been working on one of Mrs. Schmidt's dresses, but grew restless and could no longer stand the clutter. I folded the unfinished garment and put it in my sewing basket along with my pincushion, scissors, and scraps. I picked up my beautiful thimble Michael had given me for Christmas and added it to the pile. Seeing it only made me feel worse. I fluffed my featherbed and pillow and arranged them neatly, then did Grandma's too. At least I could bring order to the cabin.

Winter still held the country in a tight fist. Only a powdery soft snow fell when Thomas called for me at ten o'clock, but the leaden gray sky threatened more. I didn't worry. We could get to Bradley and back before the worst. If we hurried.

"I'm so happy you changed your mind about Ohio," I said, soon after we set out.

"Changed my mind? What do you mean? I just said that when we get married I'll work with Hogan. I meant a year or two, not forever. You'll love Ohio."

"Sounds like you have it all figured out." *What about me? Don't you care what I think?*

"I've given it a lot of thought," he replied. "We'll accumulate as much gold as possible, then I, I mean we, will sell out to Hogan. *Take the money and run? That was never what Da and Mama planned.*

"This is happening too fast. I need time to think," I said.

"Let me do the thinking. Trust me to decide what's best for us. You do trust me, don't you?"

Do I? The conversation ended when a sudden weather change forced Thomas to give his full attention to driving the buggy. The wind picked up speed, and snow swirled. When we came close to Hot Pants' cabin smoke spewing from his chimney reminded me of my unfinished business. I shuddered. On our way back I would stop and apologize. I could only guess how badly I'd hurt him. Today I'd start making everything right.

After only a mile or so the snow worsened. Wind whistled through spindly poplars and pines, and we could barely see the trail ahead. We needed to turn around. Bradley could wait.

"What do you think of your Alaska, now," Thomas asked.

I ignored his sarcasm. "I still think it's the most beautiful spot on earth. But I respect it. And that means not taking foolish chances."

"You want me to turn around? Would the intrepid young Walensky turn around?"

"Yes, he would. And we should too."

"We'll turn around if it doesn't get better soon. I have an appointment I need to keep while you shop."

What kind of appointment would make him press on in this? "Turn around," I pleaded. "We'll never make it." In four years I'd seen all kinds of Alaska weather, and this had turned into what Mama always called a hunker-down-in-front-of-the-woodstove day.

"Whatever you say." His face looked grim. The horse balked when Thomas tried to make him turn. *Just what we need. The first big blizzard this year and we're at the mercy of a skittish horse.*

We finally turned, and I saw the storm's wrath. Blowing snow completely covered the tracks we had just made. Never mind going home, we had to make it back to Hot Pants' cabin. No matter how angry he might be, he would never refuse anyone shelter in a blizzard. I thought of Grandma, at home alone and worrying about me, but what could I do? Nothing.

We inched along. My heavy parka and woolen lap robe were no match for the piercing wind. I could only think of a warm fire and Hot Pants' cabin. I tried to see his chimney smoke to gage the distance, but couldn't.

Suddenly the cabin was straight ahead. I saw the door wide open, but no smoke. Prince barked wildly.

"Hurry, Thomas! There's trouble!"

"Don't worry, he probably left and the wind blew it open."

"You think he left? In this? Anyway, Prince would have gone with him." I jumped out and ran to the cabin. "Hot Pants! Where are you?"

He must have fallen. I looked around frantically, but found no one. A pile of wood stood just inside the door. He had obviously gone for more.

"The fire burned out," said Thomas.

"Start it. I'm going outside to look for him."

"Kasey, you can't. You'll die! All you can see is white."

"I have to find him!" I turned and started out.

Thomas grabbed my shoulders and spun me around. "I won't let you do it. It's suicide!"

"Then help me!"

"No! You say he loves you. Would he want you killing yourself? You don't even know he's here."

"He's here. I know he is!" I struggled free and ran toward the door.

"Listen to me! There's nothing you can do."

"No! You listen!" I grabbed a long rope from a nail over the door and tied one end around his waist. "Start the fire."

"What are you doing? You're insane!"

"Just hold the rope. As long as I don't let go of the other end, I can follow it back."

I tried running but couldn't. Prince whimpered at my side.

"Hot Pants," I called. "I'm here! I'm coming!"

But my voice was lost in the wind. He'd never hear me. Even is he was still alive. *Don't even think that. You'll find him.*

Living in Alaska had taught me not to panic. I went in what I thought was the direction of the stable. I saw only white. Everywhere. I couldn't tell where the ground ended and the sky began. My feet were numb. Frigid wind froze my nose hairs, and it hurt to breathe.

"You have to help me, Prince. There's no one else." He ran in circles. "Stop! This is no time to play."

He moved away, but not far. I couldn't see him but heard his bark. When it grew insistent, I tried to figure where the noise came from and go in that direction. I thought I heard someone call my name, and bile rose in my throat. *All right, now it's time to panic.* Hallucinations signaled the first sign of trouble in weather like this. I tripped over something. Hot Pants! He didn't move. How long had he been here? *Please, God. He can't be dead.*

He had fallen beside a pile of straw. Stonewall Jackson lay in front of him, shielding him from the brutal wind. I took off my mitten and felt under his nostrils. Miracle! He was unconscious but breathing.

"Do something," I told myself. Frantically I covered him with straw. It wasn't much, but I had nothing else, and it would protect him some while I followed the rope back. Thomas had to help carry him inside. Whether he wanted to or not.

Then I thought I heard someone again. Another hallucination. *Please, God, no. I have to stay strong until Hot Pants is all right.*

Someone brushed against me. Michael! He knelt beside Hot Pants, feeling for a pulse.

"We have to hurry," he said. He had stopped to escape the storm too. I'd never been so happy to see anyone, but my relief turned to dismay. Thomas stood behind him.

"Where's the rope? We'll never find our way back!"

"It's all right," Michael said. "I tied it to that cottonwood on the right side of the cabin, and you still have the other end.

While we lifted Hot Pants, he continued explaining. "I tied another rope for Frye and me. He raised his arm. "See, it's tied to my wrist. If we stay together we'll be all right, and we need Frye to help."

Struggling against wind and snow, we moved him inside as carefully as could. We still didn't know how badly he had been hurt. Apparently he had gone for wood and lost his way. The stove wasn't completely cold when we first arrived, so he probably hadn't been out long. Luckily, the dry snow hadn't soaked through his clothes. The straw pile and the moose had probably saved his life. *If* he regained consciousness.

His right leg looked broken, but before anything else, we had to warm him. We wrapped him in all the blankets we could find. Then settled in to wait.

"What are we going to do?" I knew I had to pull myself together. Not for me, for Hot Pants. "He needs Doc O'Malley, and he needs him now."

"I'll go to Bradley and send him just as soon as this lets up. That leg doesn't look so good," Thomas said. "Look how swollen it is. Let's take his trousers off."

"No! We have to get him warm before we do anything else." Michael was adamant.

"Oh, pardon me," Thomas said. "Who needs Doc O'Malley? We have Doc Walensky."

"You've lived here for more than a year and you still don't know anything about survival." Michael didn't even try to hide his contempt.

"Guess not. Where smart folks live, you don't have to worry about surviving. That's just something you Alaskans do."

"At least we have sense enough to help a girl find someone in trouble."

"You think it's sensible to risk your own life? We could have all died."

"But we didn't." Michael seemed determined to have the last word.

"Stop it!" Tears splashed down my face. "Hot Pants may be dying, and all you can do is insult each other. I'm ashamed of both of you."

Michael looked contrite. "I'm sorry, Kasey. I just hate feeling so helpless."

"I know. We all do." My worst fear refused to let go. *What if he dies thinking I don't trust him. That I don't love him. I told Thomas and Michael I'm ashamed of them. Da would be ashamed of me.*

Thomas glared at us. They stopped sniping, but still eyed each other with raw hostility, and Thomas paced the cabin like a caged bear. I made coffee. The cabin slowly grew warmer, and sharp pain stabbed my feet as the numbness wore off. Eventually the storm eased.

"Let's take him to Grandma. She'll know what to do."

"That's not a bad idea," Thomas said. "Walensky, take him in your buggy. I'll go on to Bradley and send Doc. Come on, Kasey. Let's go."

"Are you crazy? I'm going with Hot Pants."

"We're all going with Hot Pants," said Michael, in an authoritative voice I'd never heard before. "Kasey, you ride with me. I've got Peter's buggy and there's a back seat. Frye, think you can manage to follow? It'll take two men to carry him in." He looked at me when he said "men."

We gently laid him on the back seat, on lap robes from both buggies. I covered him with the blankets from his cabin. That's when I noticed he wasn't wearing his Christmas scarf.

Michael didn't talk while we rode. I talked, but to someone else. *"Please, God, let him live. Please, please. I promise I'll never ask for anything again. Just please don't let him die.*

When we reached the cabin I jumped out before the buggy had even stopped.

"Grandma," I hollered. "We've brought Hot Pants. He's hurt! Bad!"

By the time I opened the door, she had already pulled back the covers on her bed. "Well Lord have mercy, don't just stand there. Bring him in!"

Chapter 15

"Lay him here. Easy! We don't know what's broken," Grandma said.

Michael and Thomas placed Hot Pants on her bed. Tears stung my eyes when I looked at his ashen face. *Is it too late? It can't be!*

"Well, you folks have everything under control. The sooner I can get to Bradley and send the doctor, the better," Thomas said.

Michael shot him a look. "By the way, Frye, I forgot to tell you I saw Emily Duncan in town this morning. She said if I saw you on the trail to tell you not to worry about coming. Said she'd understand, what with the weather and all."

"Who? Emily? Is she that girl at the Gilded Cage? She–she has a gun I'm thinking about buying." Anger, directed at Michael, flashed across Thomas' face.

"That's odd," I said. "Emily's afraid of guns."

"You don't believe me? Surely you're not jealous. What would I want with a girl like that? She's nothing but a saloon dancer."

"She's also my friend, and I refuse to listen to you say unkind things about her," I said.

"And speaking of saying unkind things, Mr. Frye," Grandma said. "Henry Hogan is a mountain man by birth, not a gentleman, but I have never met anyone more honest. I don't believe for a minute he'd cheat Kasey. Or anyone else. So stop filling her head with foolishness."

"We'll talk about this another time. I'm sorry if I've offended anyone, but I really must go to Bradley now and send Doc O'Malley." He glared at Michael.

When Dr. O'Malley finally arrived, he confirmed Hot Pants had badly broken his right leg and a few ribs as well. But something else worried him too.

"More men die of pneumonia in this country than broken bones," he said. "I'll splint his leg and we'll see how he does."

I threw together a late supper. Michael had stayed, and fetched more wood while I set the table. No one felt like eating, but we went through the motions. Just before midnight, Dr. O'Malley checked his patient once more before saying good night and promising to return the next day.

Hot Pants still hovered somewhere between life and death. Once he opened his eyes and looked around, then flailed his arms wildly. "It's you," he said, looking at me with what appeared to be disgust.

"Yes, Hot Pants. It's me. Forgive me, I beg you. I love you, and Grandma and I are going to make you well."

But he slipped back into unconsciousness. My plea went unheard.

"He hates me."

"He doesn't know what he's saying," Michael said. "He doesn't even know where he is."

"Of course not, dear," Grandma said, replacing the quilt he had thrown off in his moment of wakefulness. "He's going to be fine. I can feel it. You'll get your chance to make things right."

"He has to wake up. I couldn't stand it if he doesn't."

"From your lips to God's ear," Grandma replied.

Michael left and I washed and put away the dishes. I made myself a pallet on the floor and got ready for bed. Grandma slipped into her nightclothes too, and lay on my bunk. Neither of us slept.

Toward daybreak, he rallied again. "Don't go a-stopping the clock just yet," he said before slipping back into oblivion.

The next few days brought no improvement as Hot Pants still faded in and out of consciousness. Dr. O'Malley came each day, but there was little more he could do. My fourteenth birthday came and went, but neither Grandma nor I felt like celebrating..

"He belongs in a hospital. No offense Ma'am," he said, looking at Grandma. "I know you ladies are doing the best you can."

Grandma bristled. "You're here every day, Doctor, and Henry is warm and dry and watched over every minute you're gone. What more could a hospital do?"

"Maybe you're right. You have a knack for tending sick folks, but only the good Lord knows if he's going to make it."

"Don't say that," I begged. "Doesn't every day he lives improve his chances?"

"Kasey, I wish I could say yes, but I honestly don't know."

Then on the afternoon of the fourth day, Hot Pants opened his eyes.

"Grandma, he's awake! Really awake."

"Thank God," Grandma said.

"What in thunder am I doin' here?" he asked. He tried sitting up, but weakly eased his head back down on the pillow.

"Got myself a bear of a headache." Then he hollered in pain. "My leg! What happened to my leg?"

"It's broken, Hot Pants. Broken bad. Your ribs are too, but you're going to be all right. You went out in that terrible storm and fell. Don't you remember?"

"That's right," Grandma said. "Now just lie down and let us take care of you. I'm not letting you die, not after watching over you all this time."

"What d'ya mean? How long's it been?"

"Four days."

"Four days! Wait a minute. This ain't my shirt. These ain't my britches either."

"They're Da's clothes. We cleaned you up. Dr. O'Malley had to cut your pants off. Your leg was pretty swollen."

"You mean . . .?" He looked at Grandma and flushed.

I smiled. I'd never seen Hot Pants embarrassed before.

"Yes, you old fool, Doc O'Malley and I undressed you," Grandma said. "I nursed boys in the war. You're not the first man I've seen naked. Hope you'll be the last, though, it sure isn't a pretty sight."

"Grandma! Stop! He almost died." Then I saw tears in her eyes, and realized she was relieved too.

"Reckon I owe you my life, but how'd you git me here?"

"All I've done is take care of you. Kasey and the boys brought you here. Michael and Thomas. Kasey saved your life. She and Thomas stopped at your cabin and you weren't there. She went out looking for you. Didn't quit till she found you either."

Hot Pants eyed me intently. "You and Frye found me?"

I hesitated. "Yes. Well sort of. He had to hold the rope while I searched."

"Why wuzn't you holdin' the rope and him out lookin'? Don't bother yourself answerin' that. It's 'cause he's a yeller-belly. Sendin' a girl out in a storm…."

I vowed never to tell Hot Pants the whole truth. That Thomas not only didn't send me out, he actually tried to stop me. Had I listened, Hot Pants would have died.

"All that matters now is that we found you in time. Michael came along, and the three of us brought you here."

Grandma held a teacup up to his lips. "Sip a little of this, then go back to sleep. You'll be feeling like eating something a little later. I'll make some broth. Now you need to rest and let your bones knit."

"All right. But then I'm goin' home," Hot Pants said, but without much conviction.

"You'll leave when Dr. O'Malley and I say you can," Grandma said.

"Don't argue with her, Hot Pants, it won't do you any good."

"Toads and crocodiles!"

I took the cup from Grandma and held it as he sipped. Then Grandma went out to fetch water, leaving us alone.

"How'd you know I wuz outside?" he asked.

"Prince was barking like a banshee. I knew if he was home, you were too. And you'd fetched wood, so it looked like you had gone out for more and gotten in trouble."

"Where's Prince?"

"He's fine, Michael's keeping him until you're well."

"Only thing I don't understan' is why you wuz there in the first place."

All the strain of the last weeks lifted as I finally had my chance to apologize to this man I loved like a grandfather. "Thomas and I were heading to Bradley Pass. We turned back because of the storm." I took a deep breath and the words tumbled out. "But that's not the only reason. I planned to stop on the way home anyway. I'm so sorry I questioned you like I did." I didn't realize I was crying until I saw big wet splotches on the quilt.

"Darlin,' you're like my own flesh 'n blood. I'd never…"

"I know, Hot Pants. I didn't mean it. Can you ever forgive me?"

"That wasn't you talkin', darlin'. That was Thomas Frye. Yellerbelly!"

Chapter 16

Three weeks later I drove Hot Pants' buggy to Bradley. Longer days and morning sun promised better days ahead. I had time to think about Thomas, and how differently I felt about him since the storm.

I'd thought of him as a man. But how cowardly he'd behaved. I knew I could never marry him. He didn't even like Alaska. Now I had to find a way to tell him without hurting his feelings. *Emily. I'll talk to her. She's older and more experienced. Emily can tell me what to say.*

Also, I hoped to run into Michael. He had been to see Hot Pants a few times, but hadn't talked much to me. I needed to tell him how wrong I'd been. My mind kept going back to that day he had kissed me goodbye at Susannah's hotel. And how good that kiss had felt. I wanted him to do it again. *Was it too late?*

Despite recent warming, piles of snow still lined both sides of Front Street. "Whoa," I said to Elwood, and hitched him to the post outside the general store. I stepped inside and saw Doc O'Malley.

"Morning, Kasey. How's our patient?" He put a dozen candles on the counter, and fished a gherkin from the pickle barrel.

Benny, the storekeeper, hurried back behind the counter, eager to hear about Hot Pants. "He must be getting better. He gets grumpier every day," I said.

"An excellent sign," the doctor said.

"Tell that to Grandma. She said she's ready to break his other leg.

"Looks to me like she's enjoying every minute of it."

"You're right. You can tell her if you want to. Not me, I still have to live with her."

Truth be told, the three of us had settled into a routine. I loved those long evenings when she and Hot Pants talked of days gone by. I couldn't speak for them, but to me it felt like family. Dr. O'Malley settled his account and left. I chose my purchases: thread, soap for Grandma, and a tin of Prince Albert tobacco for Hot Pants.

Back outside, I caught myself glancing in both directions, still thinking about Michael. Then I felt guilty. *First things first. I have to talk with Emily and work up some courage. Too bad Benny doesn't sell that! Then I'll find Thomas.*

"A little while longer, Elwood," I said. I patted him, and placed my purchases on the seat.

When I stepped inside Emily's corner rooming house and into a small entrance hall, I stopped short. There she stood smiling into the eyes of a man who held her in his arms. My chest exploded. Thomas! They both turned in my direction.

"Kasey," Emily said, "how wonderful to see you!"

Thomas said something to Emily. It sounded like "shut up."

"I have to go," I blurted. Dizziness swept over me as I ran down the boardwalk.

Emily called after me. "Kasey! Are you all right?"

For a few minutes I sat shaking in the buggy. Hot Pants and Michael had been right all along. How could I have been such a goose? I wasn't jealous. Only angry with Thomas for proving again he had never been the man I'd thought. Angry with myself as well. I hate stupidity, especially when it's mine. Then relief washed over me. *It's over and I don't have to do a thing.*

"Kasey, what are you doing here? Hot Pants…?" Michael approached the buggy.

"He's fine. I'm just here to pick up a few things." His concern touched me. "You didn't ask, but I'm fine too." For the first time in a long time, I felt a smile spread across my face.

"Don't go home, now," he said. "At least have a cup of tea first."

"I thought you'd never ask." I took his hand and stepped down on the slushy street. "Sorry, Elwood," I said, and patted his mane.

Michael took a few sugar cubes from his pocket. Elwood ate them from his hand.

Soon we were seated in front of the woodstove in Susannah Prentice's dining room. It felt like a lifetime ago that Michael had kissed me at this same hotel where Grandma waited.

"Tell me about Hot Pants. I was going to stop by on my way home." He sounded friendly enough, but he avoided my eyes.

"Oh, he gets stronger every day. He still can't walk and he's getting crotchety. Grandma said he's always been that way and I just never noticed."

"She's right." He smiled. At the tabletop, not at me.

"How's Hot Pants?" Susannah asked as she placed a steaming pot of tea and some dried-apple pie on the table before sitting down with us.

Michael seemed relieved by the distraction. After Susannah had been filled in, she turned to Michael. "John came in yesterday. Said your year is up." She patted his hand. "He's so proud of you. I know he wanted you working the mine with him and Peter, but believe me, he's proud."

"What year? What are you talking about?" I gave them both a blank look.

"Nothing much," Michael said. "I started my business a year ago, that's all."

"What do you mean 'that's all?'" Susannah turned to me. "Didn't you know Michael promised John he'd work in the Sure Thing if he wasn't doing well in a year?"

I hadn't known. I realized then how much his impulsive proposal last autumn had meant. Marriage would have been a real burden, yet he had been willing to do it. For me. More customers came in and Susannah excused herself.

"You should have told me." The lump in my throat felt as big as Alaska.

"Thought I did," he muttered. "Is everything settled between you and Hot Pants?"

"Yes, I told him how wrong I'd been about so many things. He pegged Thomas right. You did too."

I watched his face, eager to see his reaction, but there was none to see. He still wasn't wearing the scarf I made him. Probably for the same reason I threw Thomas' hair clip away.

"Michael, I made a terrible mistake."

"We all make mistakes. Let's finish our pie. Elwood's tired of waiting." *That's it? I bare my soul and he's worried about Elwood?*

"You're right. I have to get home."

Chapter 17

The calendar said spring, but it hadn't quite happened. Yukon River travel was still weeks away, and melting creeks could no longer be safely crossed. Mild days caused thawing, but a freeze always followed. Oddly, now with spring almost within reach, we got cabin fever and got it bad. Visiting provided relief.

The Amundsens stopped in one morning. "We were on our way to Bradley and thought Aurora should visit her godmother," Linnea explained.

"Ya, and her honorary grandma." Nils gave Grandma a big hug.

"What 'bout me? Can't I be the hon'rary grandpa," Hot Pants asked.

"You're already mine," I said, "But I don't mind sharing."

We passed the baby from lap to lap while everyone clucked over her. Someone else knocked on the door, this time Montana Simms, an old acquaintance of Hot Pants and Da.

"Come in, come in," Grandma said. "Have a seat on Kasey's bunk. All the chairs are taken. Land sakes, we're packed in here so tight you couldn't stir us with a stick." Her eyes sparkled. She obviously loved having a cabin full of people to feed and fuss over.

I didn't know Montana, but remembered hearing Da and Hot Pants talk about him. They had met on the Chilkoot Pass the year before Da sent for Mama and me. He had staked a claim deeper in Alaska, on a Tanana River tributary. It had proved worthless, and now he decided to try again near Fortymile.

Thomas came too. *Of all the nerve! How dare he show up here acting as if nothing had happened?*

"Come on in and close the door," Grandma called out to him. "It may be April, but it still feels like winter to me."

"Yesiree, this weather's enough to give you the weary dismals," Montana agreed.

Only two days had passed since I found Thomas with Emily, and I hadn't yet confided in Grandma or Hot Pants, so I held my tongue. "Montana Sims, this is Thomas Frye. Mr. Frye stops by for coffee and a slice of Grandma's raisin pie once in a while."

Grandma raised her eyebrows, but said nothing. The look she shot me, however, told me she would demand a full explanation later. Before the interruption, Hot Pants had told Montana about the storm, and how Thomas and I arrived first at his cabin, with Michael coming just minutes later.

"So it appears this young fellow saved your life," Montana said, nodding toward Thomas.

"He helped Kasey and Michael," Hot Pants said. "You probably knew Frye's uncle, Dave West," he went on.

"Know him well, but haven't seen him in donkey years," Montana said. "A real fine fellow. Wait, did you say *knew*? He's all right, isn't he?"

"No sir, I'm sorry to say he passed away last summer," said Thomas.

"Sorry to hear it. Mining accident?"

"No, he took sick. Pneumonia, most likely."

"I'm mighty sorry. Good man. He talked big, and dreamed even bigger. Always wore that horrible orange hat." Montana smiled at the memory. "Said it would bring him luck. Guess he was wearing it when he won big in a poker game back in Leadville. Thought it would lead him to gold."

Thomas smiled too, and never saw the look passing between Hot Pants and me. My stomach tightened, and I ran outside. Grandma called after me to shut the door, but I barely heard her. I leaned against a cottonwood tree and buried my face in my hands. Soon Thomas touched my arm.

"That was your uncle in my father's grave last summer." My voice shook.

"Yes," he said. "I wanted to tell you before, but didn't want to upset you."

"No. You didn't want to tell me. If anything you were worried I'd find out."

"Kasey, it's not what you think."

"How do you know what I think?" Tears rolled down my cheeks and I made no attempt to hide them. "You turned my father's funeral into a sideshow."

"Kasey, I'm sorry. I really am."

"How did your uncle die? Did you …?"

"Did I *kill* him? Of course not. What do you think I am?"

"You don't really want me to answer that."

"No, I didn't kill him," he said, ignoring my sarcasm. "I don't know what he died of. Like I said, pneumonia probably. His fever got worse. I was going to send for the doctor as soon as someone happened by. Couldn't leave him alone long enough to go myself." I sensed he told me the truth, saw the memory still brought pain. "No one ever came so I decided to chance taking him to Bradley. It was his only hope. He died that night."

"This is nowhere near your cabin. Why did you want him buried here?"

"I didn't set out to do that. He knew he was dying and made me promise to bury him at Abernathy Creek. He passed through there on his way in. Said it was the most peaceful spot he'd ever seen."

"Then why didn't you take him there?"

"I intended to. I built a coffin, then loaded it on the wagon and set out. A wheel came loose and the coffin bounced off and splintered. Uncle Dave rolled out." I shuddered, but Thomas kept talking. "Do you know how far Abernathy Creek is?"

"Yes." Actually, I had never even heard of it, but Thomas needed to know I would not make this easy for him.

He looked at me pleadingly, obviously not wanting to continue, but knowing he had no choice. "I got to wondering what difference it made. He was already dead. Do you think he knew where I buried him?"

"I don't know the answer to that. Do you?"

"Kasey, don't make this any worse than it already is. I happened upon the grave and it just looked too good to pass up. I didn't know you yet and I certainly didn't know your father."

"But you just left him there and ran away. After you promised. What about that?"

"I swear I took good care of him right up until he died. After that, what difference did it make?"

"A promise made is a debt unpaid," I mumbled.

"What did you say?"

"Da always said a promise not kept is like a debt not paid. I remember him and Hot Pants talking about men risking their own lives in dead of winter to keep a promise to a dying friend. You couldn't even do it in summer sunshine. And Dave West was your uncle, not just a friend."

Thomas' mouth smiled, but his eyes turned cold. "I guess I'm not perfect like Hogan, or even like Michael Walensky," he said. "It's him, isn't it? You're going to marry Walensky."

"No. Maybe. I hope so. I don't even know if he still wants me."

"He wants you. That boy wants you."

"He's not a boy. I told him once that he's a boy and you're a man. I was wrong about both of you."

I shivered, suddenly aware of a chill in the air. It smelled like more snow would fall. In my haste to leave I hadn't bothered to grab my parka or boots. Now I longed for the warm woodstove, and turned to leave.

Thomas had other ideas. "Oh? You think you were wrong about me?" He grabbed my arm and pulled me back. "You think I'm not a man? I'll show you a man."

I struggled to get free. "Let me go! What do you think you're doing?"

Panting, he leaned closer and held my hands behind my back. I smelled liquor on his breath, but he wasn't drunk. Just mean. My anger turned to loathing as he kissed me roughly on my mouth. His beard scratched my face. I fought back, kicking his shin as hard as I could.

"Ow! You little . . .." As suddenly as he had grabbed me, he let me go. The fury left his face, the coldness remained. "Sorry, Kasey. I just wanted to make sure you knew how it felt to be kissed by a man. Remember this moment after you marry the kid."

"Michael's twice the man you'll ever be." I turned and ran. Thomas followed, but did not go in.

Inside, I discovered the Amundsens had left, and found Michael at the table. I hadn't seen him arrive. Had he seen me with Thomas? And if so, what had he seen?

"Where's Thomas? Least he could have done was come in and say goodbye," Grandma said.

"He won't be coming here again, Grandma. Not ever."

She turned and faced me. "Your lip! It's bleeding! What happened?"

I wiped my mouth on my sleeve. Thomas must have bitten me. I cringed. If Michael hadn't already known I was outside with Thomas, he knew it now. I glanced in his direction and caught him staring at my dress. That's when I realized Thomas had ripped the sleeve when he pulled my arm. With no privacy to change, I grabbed Grandma's shawl off the peg and wrapped it around my arms. Michael watched me but his face revealed nothing. I had to talk to him. To explain. But how? We never had a minute alone.

Chapter 18

Hot Pants remained bedridden, though Dr. O'Malley said in another six weeks he would be up and walking. Meanwhile, he grudgingly accepted his dependence on Grandma and me. He and Grandma still bickered, but I noticed their verbal battles had become almost gentle.

Me, I had a head full of cobwebs to clear. Long walks helped me think. Every day I set out as soon as I finished my morning chores. Most days I hiked along the creek and returned home hours later, exhausted. Michael still avoided me whenever he could, and I felt nothing but contempt for Thomas. What a silly goose I'd been. Hot Pants forgave me, but would my luck hold with Michael? From somewhere deep inside, I knew I'd regret it forever if we had no future together.

One day I took a different route and headed home along the main trail. I saw MacBeth and McDuff and the stopped buggy. Michael moved slowly along one side of the trail as if looking for something. He wore a tan mackinaw with his stocking cap pulled down over his ears. The coat fit his broad shoulders perfectly and his hat looked endearingly boyish.

My heart thumped, then thumped again. Since when did a coat and hat make me feel like this? *Since right now with Michael wearing them.*

"Michael! What are you doing?" His startled look told me he hadn't heard me coming.

"Be quiet, and get in the buggy. Now." he said softly.

"Why? What's going on?"

"Do as I say. There's something there. An animal." That's when I saw the rifle in his hand.

"Did you see it?"

"Just a flash of fur. Don't know if it's a wolf or a moose, or even an early bear. Get in the buggy. Now!"

Just as I did, something darted out of the underbrush. The beast turned out to be a husky. Prince.

Michael looked so embarrassed I tried not to laugh, but gave in to a fit of giggles.

"It's not funny," Michael said. Finally he laughed too. "He's never done that before. Why did he sneak through the woods? I would have let him come."

"He used to do that when Da tried to leave him home. Maybe he misses Hot Pants. Do you mind if I take him home with me," I asked.

"Why would I mind? Dumb mutt isn't even my dog. Come on, I'll take you both home."

Just what I'd been praying for. My chance to talk. Now all I had to do was figure out what to say. '*How do I go from 'How have you been?' to 'Do you think you might still want to marry me someday?'*

"Michael, I'm so sorry for what happened. Does Anna hate me?"

"Hate you? Of course not. She still hopes…" He clammed up.

"Hopes what." I asked.

"Nothing. Forget it."

I willed myself not to cry. "I don't want to forget it."

He didn't reply for a minute or two. "Ma understands," he said finally. Seeing how hard it was hard for him to talk about it made me feel even worse. "Ma said you had been through an awful time with your father and all, and Frye took advantage of you."

Bless you, Anna Walensky. "That's kind of her. But what about you?" *There. I said it.*

"I don't know," he said. "Ma said it's good you made your mistake now and got it out of your system. She said I should put my pride in my pocket and forget it ever happened." During the whole conversation he had never once looked at me.

We arrived at the cabin too soon. I got out of the buggy and so did Prince. To my surprise Michael did too. "A long time ago you told me we don't have to figure it all out today. That's still true." He patted my shoulder. "I'm going to say a quick hello to Hot Pants and your grandma and then be on my way." He hesitated. "I didn't tell you what else Ma said. She wants to kick Frye's sorry behind all the way back to Ohio."

"Tell her I know a few people who would like to help. Me included." He smiled. *At least we're still friends. But I want more. So much more.*

Blue lupine, the first wildflowers I'd seen this spring, bloomed along the creek. I picked an armload. Grandma would love them, and they would cheer the cabin when Michael came to see Hot Pants. I still didn't dare hope he'd come to see me.

"They're lovely," Grandma said, filling Mama's chipped milk glass vase with water before positioning it in the center of the table. "This whole country is beautiful. Can't believe I never noticed until now."

"You ain't had no reason till now," Hot Pants said, his eyes twinkling. "You gonna tell Kasey? Or am I?"

"Tell me what?"

"Well I am, of course." Grandma looked nervous, but her eyes were shining. "Kasey, Henry and I are going to be married."

"Married? I don't believe it! That's the best news I've ever heard! But wait a minute, you don't even like each other," I blurted, before hugging them both.

"Well thunderation, it wasn't that I didn't like her," Hot Pants said. "She was just so danged uppity when she first came here."

"Well *I* didn't like *you*. Not until I got used to you. And, Kasey, admit it, he takes some getting used to."

"She's right, Hot Pants. You do."

A few days later Linnea and I strolled along the creek. Linnea held Aurora. "You are the prettiest, smartest, most precious baby in the whole world." I said, scooping her from her mother and smothering her with kisses. "Here she is seven months old already. I can't believe it."

"Ya. You were with us when she came. I've never seen anyone as miserable as you were then. And yust look at you now," Linnea replied.

"I know. Except for my friends I had no one. And Linnea, you were so right. Family is everything. If Grandma hadn't been iced in with me, I'd never have gotten to really know her. I love her so much, I can't imagine my life without her."

"And Hot Pants will be your grandfather. Who'd have ever thought that?"

"Certainly not me." I laughed. "They hardly spoke a kind word to each other before he broke his leg. But isn't it wonderful?"

"Kasey, I can tell you now. I'm so glad you're not marrying Thomas. I had a bad feeling about him, almost from the day he showed up at Clancy's with Reverend Watson."

"Seems everyone did but me. I'd say you should have told me, but I wouldn't have listened."

"Kasey! Linnea! Wait! You have company." Grandma and Emily Duncan hurried toward us.

"Emily! Come look at this beautiful baby." I held Aurora out to her. "Say hello to Emily, sweetheart." But Aurora ignored her outstretched arms and buried her face in my neck.

"I have news," Emily said shyly, after a few minutes of polite conversation. "I'm getting married.

I stretched my lips into what I hoped passed for a smile. How could I warn my friend she was making a big mistake without it looking like jealousy.

"Well, that *is* news," I said after taking a deep breath. "I hope you and Thomas will be very happy."

"Emily…," Linnea began, a worried look creeping across her face.

"No! Not Thomas!" Emily laughed. "I used to think I loved him, but now I know all about him trying to marry you, Kasey. I know what happened with his uncle, too. He's not a bad man really. He did foolish things because he doesn't belong here."

"That's a charitable way of putting it. Anyway, you're supposed to bloom wherever God plants you," Grandma snorted. Then she laughed. "But who am I to talk? Took me a long time to take root."

"But if not Thomas, who?" I could hardly contain my curiosity.

"Ya, who's the lucky man?" Linnea asked

Emily blushed. "Edward. Dr. O'Malley."

"Dr. O'Malley! How wonderful," Grandma said.

"I went to see him after that big storm. To ask about Hot Pants. We liked each other right away and it just kept growing. Then when you found Thomas and me in the boarding house, he acted so strange I told him not to come around anymore." She took a deep breath. "Kasey, if you hadn't stopped in that day, I would have made the biggest mistake of my life."

"That day solved a lot of problems didn't it? Everything turned out well for both of us." *Or would if Michael could ever really care about me again.*

"Anyway," Emily went on, "as soon as Edward knew for sure I was free, he stated his intentions. I know he's a lot older, but I don't care. I love him with all my heart and he loves me." She giggled.

"Thomas did propose. After he knew he couldn't have you. Funny thing, he always made me feel like I wasn't quite good enough for him." Color rose in her cheeks. "Edward says he's lucky to have me. Can you imagine?" Her dark eyes shone with happiness.

"Yes, Emily, we can, because he is lucky. Bless his heart," Grandma said.

I remembered Grandma's first reaction to Emily and squeezed her hand. Hot Pants always said it takes a big person to admit to being wrong. Grandma did it gracefully.

"Emily, just so you know the truth," I said, "Thomas never really loved me. He loved my gold mine."

Chapter 19

Bright spring sunshine warmed Grandma and me as we washed clothes in the creek. Everywhere we looked buds had burst into tiny leaves.

"Land sakes, if this doesn't beat all," Grandma said as she wrung a petticoat. "At least we have a washboard and don't have to beat the clothes on rocks."

"It's not so bad," I replied. "We'll be done in no time."

"Didn't say it was bad. Just never thought I'd ever be washing my unmentionables in a creek in Alaska."

We finished the wash, then strung a rope between two trees and hung everything up to dry. I looking forward to wearing garments that smelled fresh from outdoors instead of scorched on the woodstove.

That done, we made Hot Pants an early lunch of beans and bacon. Finally we hitched Elwood and headed for Bradley Pass. The long awaited first riverboat would dock today. All winter I had dreaded this day believing Grandma would try forcing me to leave Alaska. Hot Pants' accident left him unable to do hard physical work for a few more months, so in two weeks all three of us would go Outside. First to Virginia so Grandma could sell her house and most of her belongings. Then on to Georgia to visit Hot Pants' family. Most exciting of all, Grandma would take part of the money from the sale of her house so we could all travel to Scotland and finally meet Grandma Kathleen. I looked forward to it all, knowing when we came back it would be forever.

Grandma broke the tranquil silence. "What a glorious day. That dang river is almost singing."

I stared at her in amazement. I'd never heard her say "dang," but mostly because she had fallen under the river's spell. "It *is* singing, Grandma. And listen to yourself, you sound like Hot Pants."

"One could do worse, bless his heart."

In town we learned the *Alice B.* had already docked, unloaded, and taken on a load of wood to provide steam. Departing passengers began lining up to board.

Townspeople, newcomers, and miners filled Front Street. Doors swung open in saloons and lively music floated over the crowd. We celebrated each year's first riverboat as it meant we were no longer cut off from the rest of the world. I had two letters to mail. One to Grandma Kathleen and one to Carolina Wilson, the milliner in Richmond. I hoped Miss Wilson would take me on as an apprentice while we were in Virginia this summer.

We collected our mail. I had letters and Christmas presents from Grandma Kathleen that had missed the last boat. Grandma's friends had written when she failed to return last fall. As soon as we got back home I would tear into the "wish book," my new Sears and Roebuck catalog.

Grandma stopped to visit Susannah while I milled through the crowd, hoping to see Michael. Instead, Thomas called my name.

"So, you're really staying," he said. "I was surprised to hear about your grandmother and Hogan. I wish them every happiness and I really mean that."

I hadn't seen him since that awful day he kissed me. I didn't think of it as a kiss, actually "assault" better described it. Now he acted as if that ugly scene had never happened. I followed his lead. Maybe Emily had been right and he simply couldn't handle the situation in which he found himself. Knowing I never had to see him again, I gave him the benefit of the doubt.

"Thank you," I said, looking at the battered suitcase at his feet. "And I'm not surprised you're leaving."

"Sorry, but I just can't share your enthusiasm for this miserable place." He smiled.

"There's no place I'd rather be."

"I know. You'd rather make frocks or hats, working yourself into an early grave in this hostile land. I still think you belong in a city, buying dresses, not sewing them for other women to wear."

"An early grave isn't part of my plans. And I'd rather live here, really live, than just exist somewhere else."

Passengers jostled me as the line began to move. Thomas took both my hands in his. "Goodbye, Kasey, I wish I had met you in Ohio. Be happy."

"Thank you. I already am. And you take care of yourself."

I stayed until he boarded. He waved goodbye from the deck and I waved back, feeling a momentary pang of sadness. It vanished as I realized that, exciting as thinking I was in love with Thomas had been, it had never made me happy.

"Good riddance is what I say." I turned as Dr. O'Malley touched my elbow. I laughed.

"No harm done. "Emily didn't marry him, and neither did I. By the way, congratulations! She's a wonderful person."

"I know. And I'm the luckiest man in the world."

"We're both lucky." Michael had walked up behind us. "That good-for-nothing Cheechako is leaving, and he's leaving alone."

Dr. O'Malley laughed and wandered away, leaving us alone. Or as alone as we could be with the whole town out and about.

"Do you really mean that," I asked him.

"Let's take a walk," he replied. He took my hand and we strolled a little way downstream, away from the circus-like frenzy still gripping Bradley Pass.

"Did you mean what you said back there," I asked again.

He took me in his arms and kissed me. Really kissed me, like he had that day in front of Susannah's hotel. It felt even better than I remembered.

"If that doesn't answer your question, we'll have to do it again." He smiled down at me, and I saw the old Michael. The one I love. *I do love him, and now it's the marrying kind.*

"Let's do it again, anyway."

"Don't be greedy," he teased. He held my hand again, but dropped it abruptly. "Excuse me for a minute," he said, and put his hand in his pocket. Then he took my hand again and smiled. "Decided it's time to take Ma's advice and put my pride in my pocket."

Chapter 20

"Grandma, you and Hot Pants couldn't have picked a more perfect wedding day. Not if you ordered it from Sears and Roebuck."

"It's sure enough lovely," she agreed. "And a good omen for the days ahead."

Late May sunlight warmed the clearing, and bright magenta fireweed grew in large patches beside larkspur and columbine in soft shades of pink, yellow, and white. Warblers and juncos sang unseen in the treetops. Mew gulls soared overhead, occasionally swooping down and skimming the river's surface before flying away.

Grandma wore a light blue dress I made for her. Hot Pants wore a new plaid shirt and waxed canvas trousers. They spoke their vows outside. In weather like this, no one would dream of being married in Clancy's saloon. Grandma and I had worked hard for days preparing food for the fifty people who attended. Some guests also brought food. Planks over sawhorses held stews, roasted ptarmigan, smoked salmon, beans, and the ever-present sourdough bread. Rich nutty cakes and fruit pies completed our feast. We had as much coffee as anyone wanted to drink because that first riverboat had brought everything we had run out of, even fresh eggs and butter.

"Just look at this spread. I declare I feel as rich as cream," Grandma said, after everything was in place.

"You are, Grandma. We all are in every way that matters."

Reverend Watson performed their simple ceremony. My heart burst with love and with pride as Grandma and Hot Pants promised to love and honor each other always. Grandma promised to obey too, and I didn't laugh, even though I knew that would never happen.

As John Walensky would say later, we didn't just tie a marital knot that day, but a lot of loose ends as well. He and Peter had approached Hot Pants and me a few days earlier about forming a partnership. We had already worked out the details, and signed the papers after the wedding.

Among other things, we would hire a few of the Cheechakos swarming north. That way we could get work done in both mines.

"Just sign this so it'll all be legal," John said, handing me a sheaf of papers. The papers included receipts and Da's and Hot Pants' original partnership agreement.

"Now don't go worrying yourself 'bout all that other stuff, darlin'," Hot Pants said. "This here one's the only one you need to sign."

But I kept reading, while Hot Pants squirmed with uncharacteristic agitation. Suddenly I understood why.

"Hot Pants Hogan! I trusted you to be honest with me. You weren't!"

"Kasey, what are you saying? Haven't we put all that nonsense behind us?" Grandma's face paled.

"But it's true, Grandma. See for yourself."

"Now, Kasey, don't go a-makin' a big thing outta nothin'," Hot Pants said.

"I want to see what she's talking about," Grandma said.

"Look. Here's the assayer's receipt for sixteen hundred dollars. It's what Hot Pants received for our gold last year."

"Yes, and I gave you eight hunnert. Now forgit it."

"Kasey, what are you talking about?" Michael asked. "Half of sixteen hundred is eight hundred."

Then I smiled and hugged Hot Pants. "But it says right here in their agreement that Da and Hot Pants would set aside twenty-five percent of what they earned each year toward the next year's expenses and *then* split the difference. That would have left only twelve hundred to split"

"Now I understand," Grandma said. Her eyes shone with love. "Kasey's share should have been only six hundred dollars. Wouldn't Thomas Frye be surprised to know the only person Henry cheated was himself?"

"Can't a man do sumpthin' for his granddaughter without ever'body makin' a big thing out of it?"

I hugged him again. "I wasn't your granddaughter then. You didn't even know Grandma."

"You wuz close enough. I jest wanted to do a little sumpthin' extra for Charles' girl."

Anna Walensky turned to Grandma. "Miz Camille, they say the apple doesn't fall far from the tree. Isn't it amazing how much like Rosemary Kasey is getting to be?"

Grandma's eyes misted. "You're right. If only my daughter could see her beautiful child."

I blushed. *Will I ever stop doing that?* I'm a long way from beautiful, though it did seem my hair was getting darker. Like Mama's.

"And now the mines will all be in the family," Anna went on. "What with you and Hot Pants married, and Kasey and Michael getting married when you come back."

My face burned. But as much as I hated being the object of speculation, I had no doubt whatsoever that another wedding would take place. I would then be almost fifteen. Michael hadn't proposed again, but we both knew.

He rescued me from further embarrassment by suggesting we take a walk. We strolled along the creek, and then rode the horses all the way to the Yukon River. It was still early, and it wouldn't get dark before midnight. As soon as we dismounted on the gravelly riverbank, Michael put his arm around my waist. It felt so right it sent a shiver up my spine. The river, dormant through winter, now burst with life. I looked up at Michael and was once again struck by his strength. Not just physical strength, but the strength of his character.

If Miss Wilson agreed to take me on as an apprentice, I would return to Alaska with a skill to sell. If not, I'd just have to think of something else. It took everyone's effort to survive in this raw land. But that would all come later. For now we had this shining moment and I wanted to hold it in my heart forever.

I put my arm around his waist and smiled up at him. "Wasn't it a beautiful wedding?"

"Yes. Your grandma's some lady. Hot Pants is a handful, but she'll be able to manage him." He laughed. "Funny how things turn out. When she first came here, I worried she'd take you away and I'd never see you again. Then I started hoping she would. To save you from Thomas Frye."

"Marrying Thomas was never a possibility. Not really. How could I marry someone who hates Alaska? And especially after how he acted in that storm." I shuddered. "If you hadn't come along, Hot Pants would be dead now, not married to Grandma. I could never have done it without you."

"Don't be so sure. You're quite a lady too. Anyway I was there." He smiled down at me, and in that smile I read a promise. He would always be there when I needed him, just as I would always be there when he needed me.

"There's another reason I couldn't have married Thomas," I said, blushing again, but determined to get my feelings out in the open. "You."

"I've waited a long time to hear you say that. Guess I knew it, but it's always good to hear the words." He kissed me softly on my mouth.

We hadn't talked about Thomas since that day in Bradley. Michael wasn't a flowery talker like Thomas. Michael acted. His eyes were on the future. Our future. My heart swelled with happiness.

"Listen to that river sing," he said. "She's really carrying on today, isn't she?"

My heart exploded. "Yes. And it's the sweetest music I've ever heard."